Augustine Birrell

Obiter Dicta

first series

Augustine Birrell

Obiter Dicta
first series

ISBN/EAN: 9783337423261

Printed in Europe, USA, Canada, Australia, Japan

Cover: Foto ©Andreas Hilbeck / pixelio.de

More available books at **www.hansebooks.com**

OBITER DICTA.

OBITER DICTA.

'An *obiter dictum*, in the language of the
law, is a gratuitous opinion, an individual im-
pertinence, which, whether it be wise or foolish,
right or wrong, bindeth none—not even the lips
that utter it.'

OLD JUDGE.

CHEAP EDITION.

LONDON :
ELLIOT STOCK, 62, PATERNOSTER ROW.
1896.

CONTENTS.

CARLYLE.

THE accomplishments of our race
have of late become so varied, that
it is often no easy task to assign him
whom we would judge to his proper
station among men; and yet, until
this has been done, the guns of our
criticism cannot be accurately levelled,
and as a consequence the greater
part of our fire must remain futile.
He, for example, who would essay to
take account of Mr. Gladstone, must
read much else besides Hansard; he
must brush up his Homer, and set
himself to acquire some theology.
The place of Greece in the provi-
dential order of the world, and of
laymen in the Church of England,

T

must be considered, together with a host of other subjects of much apparent irrelevance to a statesman's life. So too in the case of his distinguished rival, whose death eclipsed the gaiety of politics and banished epigram from Parliament: keen must be the critical faculty which can nicely discern where the novelist ended and the statesman began in Benjamin Disraeli.

Happily, no such difficulty is now before us. Thomas Carlyle was a writer of books, and he was nothing else. Beneath this judgment he would have winced, but have remained silent, for the facts are so.

Little men sometimes, though not perhaps so often as is taken for granted, complain of their destiny, and think they have been hardly treated, in that they have been allowed to remain so undeniably small; but great men, with hardly an exception, nauseate their great-

ness, for not being of the particular sort they most fancy. The poet
Gray was passionately fond, so his
biographers tell us, of military history; but he took no Quebec. General Wolfe took Quebec, and whilst
he was taking it, recorded the fact
that he would sooner have written
Gray's ' Elegy'; and so Carlyle—who
panted for action, who hated elo-
quence, whose heroes were Cromwell and Wellington, Arkwright and
the ' rugged Brindley,' who beheld
with pride and no ignoble envy the
bridge at Auldgarth his mason-father
had helped to build half a century
before, and then exclaimed, ' A noble
craft, that of a mason; a good build-
ing will last longer than most books
—than one book in a million '; who
despised men of letters, and abhorred
the ' reading public'; whose gospel
was Silence and Action—spent his
life in talking and writing; and his

legacy to the world is thirty-four volumes octavo.

There is a familiar melancholy in this; but the critic has no need tr grow sentimental. We must have men of thought as well as men ol action : poets as much as generals; authors no less than artizans; libraries at least as much as militia ; and therefore we may accept and proceed critically to examine Carlyle's thirty-four volumes, remaining somewhat indifferent to the fact that had he had the fashioning of his own destiny, we should have had at his hands blows instead of books.

Taking him, then, as he was—a man of letters—perhaps the best type of such since Dr. Johnson died in Fleet Street, what are we to say of his thirty-four volumes?

In them are to be found criticism, oiography, history, politics, poetry, and religion. I mention this variety because of a foolish notion, at one time often found suitably lodged in heads otherwise empty, that Carlyle was a passionate old man, dominated by two or three extravagant ideas, to which he was for ever giving utterance in language of equal extravagance. The thirty-four volumes octavo render this opinion untenable by those who can read. Carlyle cannot be killed by an epigram, nor can the many influences that moulded him be referred to any single source. The rich banquet his genius has spread for us is of many courses. The fire and fury of the Latter-Day pamphlets may be disregarded by the peaceful soul, and the preference given to the ' Past ' of ' Past and Present,' which, with its intense and sympathetic mediæval-ism, might have been written by a Tractarian. The ' Life of Sterling ' is the favourite book of many who would sooner pick oakum than read 'Frederick the Great' all through; whilst the mere student of *belles lettres* may attach importance to the essays on Johnson, Burns, and Scott, on Voltaire and Diderot, on Goethe and Novalis, and yet remain blankly indifferent to 'Sartor Resartus' and the 'French Revolution.'

But true as this is, it is none the less true that, excepting possibly the 'Life of Schiller,' Carlyle wrote nothing not clearly recognisable as his. All his books are his very own —bone of his bone, and flesh of his flesh. They are not stolen goods, nor elegant exhibitions of recently and hastily acquired wares.

This being so, it may be as well if, before proceeding any further, I attempt, with a scrupulous regard to brevity, to state what I take to be the invariable indications of Mr. Carlyle's literary handiwork—the tokens of his presence—'Thomas Carlyle, his mark.'

First of all, it may be stated, without a shadow of a doubt, that he is one of those who would sooner be wrong with Plato than right with Aristotle; in one word, he is a mystic. What he says of Novalis may with equal truth be said of himself: 'He belongs to that class of persons who do not recognise the syllogistic method as the chief organ for investigating truth, or feel themselves bound at all times to stop short where its light fails them. Many of his opinions he would despair of proving in the most patient court of law, and would remain well content that they should be disbelieved there.' In philosophy we shall not be very far wrong if we rank Carlyle as a follower of Bishop Berkeley; for an idealist he undoubtedly was. 'Matter,' says he, 'exists only spiritually, and to represent some idea, and body it forth. Heaven and Earth are but the time-vesture of the Eternal. The Universe is but one vast symbol of God; nay, if thou wilt have it, what is man himself but a symbol of God? Is not all that he does symbolical, a revelation to sense of the mystic God-given force that is in him?—a gospel of Freedom, which he, the " Messias of Nature," preaches as he can by act and word.' 'Yes, Friends,' he elsewhere observes, ' not our logical mensurative faculty, but our imaginative one, is King over us, I might say Priest and Prophet, to lead us heaven-ward, or magician and wizard to lead us hellward. The understand-ing is indeed thy window—too clear thou canst not make it; but phantasy is thy eye, with its colour-giving retina, healthy or diseased.' It would be easy to multiply instances of this, the most obvious and interesting trait of Mr. Carlyle's writing ; but I must bring my remarks upon it to a close by reminding you of his two favourite quotations, which have both significance. One from Shakespeare's *Tempest:*

> ' We are such stuff
> As dreams are made of, and our little life
> Is rounded with a sleep ;'

the other, the exclamation of the Earth-spirit, in Goethe's *Faust:*

> ' 'Tis thus at the roaring loom of Time I ply,
> And weave for God the garment thou seest Him
> by.'

But this is but one side of Carlyle. There is another as strongly marked, which is his second note; and that is what he somewhere calls ' his stubborn realism.' The combination of the two is as charming as it is rare. No one at all acquainted with his writings can fail to remember his almost excessive love of detail;

his lively taste for facts, simply as facts. Imaginary joys and sorrows may extort from him nothing but grunts and snorts; but let him only worry out for himself, from that great dust-heap called 'history,' some undoubted fact of human and tender interest, and, however small it may be, relating possibly to some one hardly known, and playing but a small part in the events he is recording, and he will wax amazingly sentimental, and perhaps shed as many real tears as Sterne or Dickens do sham ones over their figments. This realism of Carlyle's gives a great charm to his histories and biographies. The amount he tells you is something astonishing — no platitudes, no rigmarole, no commonform, articles which are the staple of most biography, but, instead of them, all the facts and features of the case—pedigree, birth, father

and mother, brothers and sisters,
education, physiognomy, personal
habits, dress, mode of speech ; nothing escapes him. It was a characteristic criticism of his, on one of
Miss Martineau's American books,
that the story of the way Daniel
Webster used to stand before the
fire with his hands in his pockets
was worth all the politics, philosophy, political economy, and socio-
logy to be found in other portions of
the good lady's writings. Carlyle's
eye was indeed a terrible organ : he
saw everything. Emerson, writing
to him, says : ' I think you see as
pictures every street, church, Parlia-
ment-house, barracks, baker's shop,
mutton-stall, forge, wharf, and ship,
and whatever stands, creeps, rolls,
or swims thereabout, and make all
your own.' He crosses over, one
rough day, to Dublin ; and he jots
down in his diary the personal

appearance of some unhappy creatures he never saw before or expected
to see again; how men laughed, cried,
swore, were all of huge interest to
Carlyle. Give him a fact, he loaded
you with thanks ; propound a theory,
you were rewarded with the most
vivid abuse.

This intense love for, and faculty
of perceiving, what one may call the
'concrete picturesque,' accounts for
his many hard sayings about fiction
and poetry.   He could not understand people being at the trouble of
inventing characters and situations
when history was full of men and
women ; when streets were crowded
and continents were being peopled
under their very noses. Emerson's
sphynx-like utterances irritated him
at times, as they well might ; his
orations and the like. 'I long,' he
says, 'to see some *concrete thing,*
some Event—Man's Life, American

Forest, or piece of Creation which this Emerson loves and wonders at, well *Emersonized*, depicted by Emerson—filled with the life of Emerson, and cast forth from him then to live by itself.'* But Carlyle forgot the sluggishness of the ordinary imagination, and, for the moment, the stupendous dulness of the ordinary historian. It cannot be matter for surprise that people prefer Smollett's ' Humphrey Clinker ' to his ' History of England.'

* One need scarcely add, nothing of the sort ever proceeded from Emerson. How should it? Where was it to come from ? When, to employ language of Mr. Arnold's own, ' any poor child of nature' overhears the author of ' Essays in Criticism' telling two worlds that Emerson's ' Essays' are the most valuable prose contributions to the literature of the century, his soul is indeed filled ' with an unutterable sense of lamentation and mourning and woe.' Mr. Arnold's silence was once felt to be provoking. Wordsworth's lines kept occurring to one's mind—

> ' Poor Matthew, all his frolics o'er,
> Is silent as a standing pool.'

But it was better so.

The third and last mark to which I call attention is his humoui. Nowhere, surely, in the whole field of English literature, Shakespeare excepted, do you come upon a more abundant vein of humour than Carlyle's, though I admit that the quality of the ore is not of the finest. His every production is bathed in humour. This must never be, though it often has been, forgotten. He is not to be taken literally. He is always a humourist, not unfrequently a writer of burlesque, and occasionally a buffoon.

Although the spectacle of Mr Swinburne taking Mr. Carlyle to task, as he recently did, for indelicacy, has an oddity all its own, so far as I am concerned I cannot but concur with this critic in thinking that Carlyle has laid himself open, particularly in his 'Frederick the Great,' to the charge one usually associates with the great and terrible name of Dean Swift ; but it is the Dean with a difference, and the difference is all in Carlyle's favour. The former deliberately pelts you with dirt, as did in old days gentlemen electors their parliamentary candidates; the latter only occasionally splashes you, as does a public vehicle pursuing on a wet day its uproarious course.

These, then, I take to be Carlyle's three principal marks or notes : mysticism in thought, realism in description, and humour in both.

To proceed now to his actual literary work.

First, then, I would record the fact that he was a great critic, and this at a time when our literary criticism was a scandal. He more than any other has purged our vision and widened our horizons in this great matter. He taught us there

was no sort of finality, but only nonsense, in that kind of criticism which
was content with laying down some
foreign masterpiece with the observation that it was not suited for
the English taste. He was, if not
the first, almost the first critic, who
pursued in his criticism the historical
method, and sought to make us
understand what we were required
to judge. It has been said that
Carlyle's criticisms are not final, and
that he has not said the last word
about Voltaire, Diderot, Richter, and
Goethe. I can well believe it. But
reserving 'last words' for the use of
the last man (to whom they would
appear to belong), it is surely something to have said the *first* sensible
words uttered in English on these
important subjects. We ought not
to forget the early days of the
Foreign and Quarterly Review. We
have critics now, quieter, more re-

poseful souls, taking their ease on Zion, who have entered upon a world ready to welcome them, whose keen rapiers may cut velvet better than did the two-handed broadsword of Carlyle, and whose later date may enable them to discern what their forerunner failed to perceive; but when the critics of this century come to be criticized by the critics of the next, an honourable, if not the highest place will be awarded to Carlyle.

Turn we now to the historian and biographer. History and biography much resemble one another in the pages of Carlyle, and occupy more than half his thirty-four volumes; nor is this to be wondered at, since they afford him fullest scope for his three strong points—his love of the wonderful; his love of telling a story, as the children say, ' from the very beginning;' and his humour. His

2

view of history is sufficiently lofty.
History, says he, is the true epic
poem, a universal divine scripture
whose plenary inspiration no one out
of Bedlam shall bring into question.
Nor is he quite at one with the
ordinary historian as to the true historical method. 'The time seems
coming when he who sees no world
but that of courts and camps, and
writes only how soldiers were drilled
and shot, and how this ministerial
conjurer out-conjured that other,
and then guided, or at least held,
something which he called the
rudder of Government, but which
was rather the spigot of Taxation,
wherewith in place of steering he
could tax, will pass for a more or less
instructive Gazetteer, but will no
longer be called an Historian.'

Nor does the philosophical method
of writing history please him any
better :

'Truly if History is Philosophy teaching by examples, the writer fitted to compose history is hitherto an unknown man. Better were it that mere earthly historians should lower such pretensions, more suitable for omniscience than for human science, and aiming only at some picture of the things acted, which picture itself will be a poor approximation, leave the inscrutable purport of them an acknowledged secret—or at most, in reverent faith, pause over the mysterious vestiges of Him whose path is in the great deep of Time, whom History indeed reveals, but only all History and in Eternity will clearly reveal.'

This same transcendental way of looking at things is very noticeable in the following view of Biography : 'For, as the highest gospel was a Biography, so is the life of every good man still an indubitable gospel, and preaches to the eye and heart and whole man, so that devils even must believe and tremble, these gladdest tidings. Man is heaven-born—not the thrall of circumstances, of necessity, but the victorious subduer thereof.' These, then, being his views, what are we to say of his works? His three principal historical works are, as everyone knows, ' Cromwell,'[3] The French Revolution,' and 'Frederick the Great,' though there is a very considerable amount of other historical writing scattered up and down his works. But what are we to say of these three? Is he, by virtue of them, entitled to the rank and influence of a great historian? What have we a right to demand of an historian? First, surely, stern veracity, which implies not merely knowledge but honesty. An historian stands in a fiduciary position towards his readers, and if he withholds from them important facts likely to influence their judgment, he is guilty of fraud, and, when justice is done in this world, will be condemned to refund all moneys he has made by his false professions, with compound interest. This sort of fraud is unknown to the law, but to nobody else. 'Let me know the facts!' may well be the agonized cry of the student who finds himself floating down what Arnold has called 'the vast Mississippi of falsehood, History.' Secondly comes a catholic temper and way of looking at things. The historian should be a gentleman and possess a moral breadth of temperament. There should be no bitter protesting spirit about him. He should remember the world he has taken upon himself to write about is a large place, and that nobody set him up over us. Thirdly, he must be a born story-teller. If he is not this, he has mistaken his vocation He may be a great philosopher, a useful editor, a profound scholar, and anything else his friends like to call him, except a great historian. How does Carlyle meet these requirements? His veracity, that is, his laborious accuracy, is admitted by the only persons competent to form an opinion, namely, independent investigators who have followed in his track; but what may be called the internal evidence of the case also supplies a strong proof of it. Carlyle was, as everyone knows, a hero-worshipper. It is part of his mysticism. With him man, as well as God, is a spirit, either of good or evil, and as such should be either worshipped or reviled. He is never himself till he has discovered or invented a hero; and, when he has got him, he tosses and dandles him as a mother her babe. This is a terrible

temptation to put in the way of an
historian, and few there be who are
found able to resist it. How easy to
keep back an ugly fact, sure to be a
stumbling-block in the way of weak
brethren ! Carlyle is above suspicion
in this respect. He knows no reticence. Nothing restrains him ; not
even the so-called proprieties of
history. He may, after his bois-
terous fashion, pour scorn upon you
for looking grave, as you read in his
vivid pages of the reckless manner in
which too many of his heroes drove
coaches-and-six through the Ten
Commandments. As likely as not
he will call you a blockhead, and tell
you to close your wide mouth and
cease shrieking. But, dear me! hard
words break no bones, and it is an
amazing comfort to know the facts.
Is he writing of Cromwell ?—down
goes everything—letters, speeches,
as they were written, as they were

delivered. Few great men are edited after this fashion. Were they to be so—Luther, for example—many eyes would be opened very wide. Nor does Carlyle fail in comment. If the Protector makes a somewhat distant allusion to the Barbadoes, Carlyle is at your elbow to tell you it means his selling people to work as slaves in the West Indies. As for Mirabeau, 'our wild Gabriel Honoré,' well! we are told all about him; nor is Frederick let off a single absurdity or atrocity. But when we have admitted the veracity, what are we to say of the catholic temper, the breadth of temperament, the wide Shakespearian tolerance? Carlyle ought to have them all. By nature he was tolerant enough; so true a humourist could never be a bigot. When his war-paint is not on, a child might lead him. His judgments are gracious, chivalrous, tinged with a kindly melancholy and divine pity. But this mood is never for long. Some gadfly stings him: he seizes his tomahawk and is off on the trail. It must sorrowfully be admitted that a long life of opposition and indigestion, of fierce warfare with cooks and Philistines, spoilt his temper, never of the best, and made him too often contemptuous, savage, unjust. His language then becomes unreasonable, unbearable, bad. Literature takes care of herself. You disobey her rules: well and good, she shuts her door in your face; you plead your genius: she replies, 'Your temper,' and bolts it. Carlyle has deliberately destroyed, by his own wilfulness, the value of a great deal he has written. It can never become classical. Alas! that this should be true of too many eminent Englishmen of our time. Language such as was, at one time, almost habitual with Mr. Ruskin, is a national humiliation, giving point to the Frenchman's sneer as to our distinguishing literary characteristic being '*la brutalité.*' In Carlyle's case much must be allowed for his rhetoric and humour. In slang phrase, he always 'piles it on.' Does a bookseller misdirect a parcel, he exclaims, 'My malison on all Blockheadisms and Torpid Infidelities of which this world is full.' Still, all allowances made, it is a thousand pities; and one's thoughts turn away from this stormy old man and take refuge in the quiet haven of the Oratory at Birmingham, with his great Protagonist, who, throughout an equally long life spent in painful controversy, and wielding weapons as terrible as Carlyle's own, has rarely forgotten to be urbane, and whose every sentence is a 'thing of beauty.' It must, then, be owned that too many of Carlyle's literary achievements 'lack a gracious somewhat.' By force of his genius he 'smites the rock and spreads the water;' but then, like Moses, 'he desecrates, belike, the deed in doing.'

Our third requirement was, it may be remembered, the gift of the story-teller. Here one is on firm ground. Where is the equal of the man who has told us the story of 'The Diamond Necklace'?

It is the vogue, nowadays, to sneer at picturesque writing. Professor Seeley, for reasons of his own, appears to think that whilst politics, and, I presume religion, may be made as interesting as you please, history should be as dull as possible. This, surely, is a jaundiced view. If there is one thing it is legitimate to make more interesting than another, it is the varied record of man's life upon earth. So long as we have human hearts and await

human destinies, so long as we are
alive to the pathos, the dignity, the
comedy of human life, so long shall
we continue to rank above the philosopher, higher than the politician,
the great artist, be he called drama-
tist or historian, who makes us con-
scious of the divine movement of
events, and of our fathers who were
before us. Of course we assume
accuracy and labour in our animated
historian; though, for that matter,
other things being equal, I prefer a
lively liar to a dull one.

Carlyle is sometimes as irresistible
as 'The Campbells are Coming,' or
'Auld Lang Syne.' He has described some men and some events
once and for all, and so takes his
place with Thucydides, Tacitus and
Gibbon. Pedants may try hard to
forget this, and may in their laboured
nothings seek to ignore the author
of 'Cromwell' and the 'French Re-

volution'; but as well might the
pedestrian in Cumberland or Inver-
ness seek to ignore Helvellyn or Ben
Nevis. Carlyle is *there*, and will
remain there, when the pedant of
to-day has been superseded by the
pedant of to-morrow.

Remembering all this, we are apt
to forget his faults, his eccentricities,
and vagaries, his buffooneries, his
too-outrageous cynicisms and his too-
intrusive egotisms, and to ask ourselves—if it be not this man, who is
it then to be? Macaulay, answer
some; and Macaulay's claims are not
of the sort to go unrecognised in a
world which loves clearness of expression and of view only too well. Macaulay's position never admitted of
doubt. We know what to expect,
and we always get it. It is like the
old days of W. G. Grace's cricket.
We went to see the leviathan slog
for six, and we saw it. We expected

him to do it, and he did it. So with Macaulay—the good Whig, as he takes up the History, settles himself down in his chair, and knows it is going to be a bad time for the Tories. Macaulay's style—his much-praised style—is ineffectual for the purpose of telling the truth about anything. It is splendid, but *splendide mendax,* and in Macaulay's case the style was the man. He had enormous knowledge, and a noble spirit; his knowledge enriched his style and his spirit consecrated it to the service of Liberty. We do well to be proud of Macaulay; but we must add that, great as was his knowledge, great also was his ignorance, which was none the less ignorance because it was wilful; noble as was his spirit, the range of subject over which it energized was painfully restricted. He looked out upon the world, but, behold, only the Whigs were good.

Luther and Loyola, Cromwell and
Claverhouse, Carlyle and Newman—
they moved him not; their enthusi-
asms were delusions, and their politics demonstrable errors. Whereas,
of Lord Somers and Charles first
Earl Grey it is impossible to speak
without emotion. But the world
does not belong to the Whigs; and
a great historian must be capable of
sympathizing both with delusions and
demonstrable errors. Mr. Gladstone
has commented with force upon what
he calls Macaulay's invincible ignorance, and further says that to certain aspects of a case (particularly
those aspects most pleasing to Mr.
Gladstone) Macaulay's mind was
hermetically sealed. It is difficult
to resist these conclusions; and it
would appear no rash inference from
them, that a man in a state of invincible ignorance and with a mind
hermetically sealed, whatever else he

may be—orator, advocate, statesman, journalist, man of letters—can never be a great historian. But, indeed, when one remembers Macaulay's limited range of ideas : the common-placeness of his morality, and of his descriptions ; his absence of humour, and of pathos—for though Miss Martineau says she found one pathetic passage in the History, I have often searched for it in vain ; and then turns to Carlyle—to his almost be- wildering affluence of thought, fancy, feeling, humour, pathos—his biting pen, his scorching criticism, his world-wide sympathy (save in certain moods) with everything but the smug commonplace—to prefer Macaulay to him, is like giving the preference to Birket Foster over Salvator Rosa But if it is not Macaulay, who is it to be ? Mr. Hepworth Dixon or Mr. Froude ? Of Bishop Stubbs and Professor Freeman it behoves every ignoramus to speak with respect. Horny-handed sons of toil, they are worthy of their wage. Carlyle has somewhere struck a distinction between the historical artist and the historical artizan. The bishop and the professor are historical artizans; artists they are not—and the great historian is a great artist.

England boasts two such artists. Edward Gibbon and Thomas Carlyle. The elder historian may be compared to one of the great Alpine roadways— sublime in its conception, heroic in its execution, superb in its magnificent uniformity of good workmanship. The younger resembles one of his native streams, pent in at times between huge rocks, and tormented into foam, and then effecting its escape down some precipice, and spreading into cool expanses below ; but however varied may be its fortunes—however startling its

changes—always in motion, always
in harmony with the scene around.
Is it gloomy ? It is with the gloom
of the thunder-cloud. Is it bright ?
It is with the radiance of the sun.

It is with some consternation that
I approach the subject of Carlyle's
politics. One handles them as does
an inspector of police a parcel reported to contain dynamite. The
Latter Day Pamphlets might not
unfitly be labelled ' Dangerous Ex-
plosives.'

In this matter of politics there
were two Carlyles; and, as generally
happens in such cases, his last state
was worse than his first. Up to
1843, he not unfairly might be called
a Liberal—of uncertain vote it may
be—a man difficult to work with, and
impatient of discipline, but still aglow
with generous heat ; full of large-
hearted sympathy with the poor and
oppressed, and of intense hatred of

the cruel and shallow sophistries that then passed for maxims, almost for axioms, of government. In the year 1819, when the yeomanry round Glasgow was called out to keep down some dreadful monsters called ' Radicals,' Carlyle describes how he met an advocate of his acquaintance hurrying along, musket in hand, to his drill on the Links. ' You should have the like of this,' said he, cheerily patting his gun. ' Yes,' was the reply, ' but I haven't yet quite settled on which side.' And when he did make his choice, on the whole he chose rightly. The author of that noble pamphlet ' Chartism,' published in 1840, was at least once a Liberal. Let me quote a passage that has stirred to effort many a generous heart now cold in death : ' Who would suppose ' that Education were a thing which ' had to be advocated on the ground ' of local expediency, or indeed on any

'ground? As if it stood not on the
'basis of an everlasting duty, as a
'prime necessity of man! It is a
'thing that should need no advocat-
'ing; much as it does actually need.
'To impart the gift of thinking to
'those who cannot think, and yet who
'could in that case think: this, one
'would imagine, was the first function
'a government had to set about dis-
'charging. Were it not a cruel thing
'to see, in any province of an empire,
'the inhabitants living all mutilated
'in their limbs, each strong man
'with his right arm lamed? How
'much crueller to find the strong soul
'with its eyes still sealed—its eyes
'extinct, so that it sees not! Light
'has come into the world; but to this
'poor peasant it has come in vain.
'For six thousand years the sons of
'Adam, in sleepless effort, have been
'devising, doing, discovering; in mys-
'terious, infinite, indissoluble com-

munion, warring, a little band of
' brothers, against the black empire
' of necessity and night; they have
' accomplished such a conquest and
' conquests; and to this man it is all
' as if it had not been. The four-
and-twenty letters of the alphabet
are still runic enigmas to him. He
' passes by on the other side; and
' that great spiritual kingdom, the toil-
' won conquest of his own brothers, all
' that his brothers have conquered,
' is a thing not extant for him. An
' invisible empire; he knows it not—
' suspects it not. And is not this his
' withal; the conquest of his own
' brothers, the lawfully acquired pos-
' session of all men? Baleful enchant-
' ment lies over him, from generation
' to generation; he knows not that
' such an empire is his—that such an
' empire is his at all . . . Heavier
' wrong is not done under the sun. It
' lasts from year to year, from century

'to century; the blinded sire slaves
'himself out, and leaves a blinded son;
'and men, made in the image of God,
'continue as two-legged beasts of
'labour: and in the largest empire
'of the world it is a debate whether
'a small fraction of the revenue of
'one day shall, after thirteen cen-
'turies, be laid out on it, or not laid
'out on it. Have we governors?
'Have we teachers? Have we had
a Church these thirteen hundred
'years? What is an overseer of souls,
'an archoverseer, archiepiscopus? Is
'he something? If so, let him lay
'his hand on his heart and say what
'thing!'

Nor was the man who in 1843
wrote as follows altogether at sea in
politics:

'Of Time Bill, Factory Bill, and
'other such Bills, the present editor
'has no authority to speak. He
'knows not, it is for others than he

'to know, in what specific ways it
'may be feasible to interfere with
'legislation between the workers and
'the master-workers — knows only
'and sees that legislative interference,
'and interferences not a few, are in-
'dispensable.   Nay, interference has
'begun; there are already factory in-
'spectors.   Perhaps there might be
'mine inspectors too.   Might there
'not be furrow-field inspectors withal,
'to ascertain how, on 7s. 6d. a week,
'a human family does live ?   Again,
'are not sanitary regulations possible
'for a legislature ?   Baths, free air,
'a wholesome temperature, ceilings
'twenty feet high, might be ordained
'by Act of Parliament in all establish-
'ments licensed as mills.   There are
'such mills already extant—honour
'to the builders of them.   The legis-
'lature can say to others, "Go you
'"and do likewise — better if you
'" can."'

By no means a bad programme for 1843; and a good part of it has been carried out, but with next to no aid from Carlyle.

The Radical party has struggled on as best it might, without the author of ' Chartism ' and ' The French Revolution '—

'They have marched prospering, not through his presence ;

and it is no party spirit that leads one to regret the change of mind which prevented the later public life of this great man, and now the memory of it, from being enriched with something better than a five-pound note for Governor Eyre.

But it could not be helped. What brought about the rupture was his losing faith in the ultimate destiny of man upon earth. No more terrible loss can be sustained. It is of both

heart and hope. He fell back upon
heated visions of heaven-sent heroes,
devoting their early days for the most
part to hoodwinking the people, and
their latter ones, more heroically, to
shooting them.

But it is foolish to quarrel with
results, and we may learn something
even from the later Carlyle. We lay
down John Bright's Reform Speeches,
and take up Carlyle and light upon
a passage like this : ' Inexpressibly
delirious seems to me the puddle
of Parliament and public upon what
it calls the Reform Measure, that is
to say, the calling in of new supplies
of blockheadism, gullibility, bribability, amenability to beer and
balderdash, by way of amending the
woes we have had from previous
supplies of that bad article.' This
view must be accounted for as well
as Mr. Bright's. We shall do well
to remember, with Carlyle, that the

best of all Reform Bills is that which
each citizen passes in his own breast,
where it is pretty sure to meet with
strenuous opposition.   The reform
of ourselves is no doubt an heroic
measure never to be overlooked, and,
in the face of accusations of gullibility, bribability, amenability to
beer and balderdash, our poor
humanity can only stand abashed,
and feebly demur to the bad English
in which the charges are conveyed.
But we can't all lose hope.   We remember Sir David Ramsay's reply to
Lord Rea, once quoted by Carlyle
himself.   Then said his lordship:
' Well, God mend all.' ' Nay, by God,
Donald, we must help Him to mend
it !'   It is idle to stand gaping at the
heavens, waiting to feel the thong
of some hero of questionable morals
and robust conscience; and therefore, unless Reform Bills can be
shown to have checked purity of elec-

tion, to have increased the stupidity of electors, and generally to have promoted corruption—which notoriously they have not—we may allow Carlyle to make his exit ' swearing,' and regard their presence in the Statute Book, if not with rapture, at least with equanimity.

But it must not be forgotten that the battle is still raging—the issue is still uncertain. Mr. Froude is still free to assert that the '*postmortem*' will prove Carlyle was right. His political sagacity no reader of 'Frederick' can deny; his insight into hidden causes and far-away effects was keen beyond precedent— nothing he ever said deserves contempt, though it may merit anger. If we would escape his conclusion, we must not altogether disregard his premises. Bankruptcy and death are the final heirs of imposture and make-believes. The old faiths and forms are worn too threadbare by a thousand disputations to bear the burden of the new democracy, which, if it is not merely to win the battle but to hold the country, must be ready with new faiths and forms of her own. They are within her reach if she but knew it; they lie to her hand: surely they will not escape her grasp! If they do not, then, in the glad day when worship is once more restored to man, he will with becoming generosity forget much that Carlyle has written, and remembering more, rank him amongst the prophets of humanity.

Carlyle's poetry can only be exhibited in long extracts, which would be here out of place, and might excite controversy as to the meaning of words, and draw down upon me the measureless malice of the metricists. There are, however, passages in 'Sartor Resartus' and the 'French

Revolution' which have long appeared to me to be the sublimest
poetry of the century; and it was
therefore with great pleasure that I
found Mr. Justice Stephen, in his
book on 'Liberty, Equality, and
Fraternity,' introduciug a quotation
from the 8th chapter of the 3rd
book of 'Sartor Resartus,' with the
remark that 'it is perhaps the most
memorable utterance of the greatest
poet of the age.'

As for Carlyle's religion, it may
be said he had none, inasmuch as
he expounded no creed and put his
name to no confession. This is the
pedantry of the schools. He taught
us religion, as cold water and fresh
air teach us health, by rendering
the conditions of disease well nigh
impossible. For more than half a
century, with superhuman energy,
he struggled to establish the basis
of all religions, 'reverence and godly

fear.' ' Love not pleasure, love God; this is the everlasting Yea.'

One's remarks might here naturally come to an end, with a word or two of hearty praise of the brave course of life led by the man who awhile back stood the acknowledged head of English letters. But the present time is not the happiest for a panegyric on Carlyle. It would be in vain to deny that the brightness of his reputation underwent an eclipse, visible everywhere, by the publication of his ' Reminiscences.' They surprised most of us, pained not a few, and hugely delighted that ghastly crew, the wreckers of humanity, who are never so happy as when employed in pulling down great reputations to their own miserable levels. When these ' baleful creatures,' as Carlyle would have called them, have lit upon any passage indicative of conceit or jealousy or spite, they have fastened upon it and screamed over it, with a pleasure but ill-concealed and with a horror but ill-feigned. ' Behold,' they exclaim, ' your hero robbed of the nimbus his inflated style cast around him—this preacher and fault-finder reduced to his principal parts : and lo ! the main ingredient is most unmistakably " bile !" '

The critic, however, has nought to do either with the sighs of the sorrowful, ' mourning when a hero falls,' or with the scorn of the malicious, rejoicing, as did Bunyan's Juryman, Mr. Live-loose, when Faithful was condemned to die : ' I could never endure him, for he would always be condemning my way.'

The critic's task is to consider the book itself, *i.e.,* the nature of its contents, and how it came to be written at all.

When this has been done, there will not be found much demanding moral censure ; whilst the reader will note with delight, applied to the trifling concerns of life, those extraordinary gifts of observation and apprehension which have so often charmed him in the pages of history and biography.

These peccant volumes contain but four sketches : one of his father, written in 1832 ; the other three, of Edward Irving, Lord Jeffrey, and Mrs. Carlyle, all written after the death of the last-named, in 1866.

The only fault that has been found with the first sketch is, that in it Carlyle hazards the assertion that Scotland does not now contain his father's like. It ought surely to be possible to dispute this opinion without exhibiting emotion. To think well of their forbears is one of the few weaknesses of Scotchmen. This sketch, as a whole, must be carried to Carlyle's credit, and is a permanent addition to literature. It is pious, after the high Roman fashion. It satisfies our finest sense of the fit and proper. Just exactly so should a literate son write of an illiterate peasant father. How immeasurable seems the distance between the man from whom proceeded the thirty-four volumes we have been writing about and the Calvinistic mason who didn't even know his Burns!—and yet here we find the whole distance spanned by filial love.

The sketch of Lord Jeffrey is inimitable. One was getting tired of Jeffrey, and prepared to give him the go-by, when Carlyle creates him afresh, and, for the first time, we see the bright little man bewitching us by what he is, disappointing us by what he is not. The spiteful remarks

4

the sketch contains may be considered, along with those of the
same nature to be found only too
plentifully in the remaining two
papers.

After careful consideration of the
worst of these remarks, Mrs.
Oliphant's explanation seems the
true one; they are most of them
sparkling bits of Mrs. Carlyle's conversation. She, happily for herself,
had a lively wit, and, perhaps not so
happily, a biting tongue, and was, as
Carlyle tells us, accustomed to make
him laugh, as they drove home
together from London crushes, by
far from genial observations on
her fellow-creatures, little recking—
how should she?—that what was so
lightly uttered was being engraven
on the tablets of the most marvellous
of memories, and was destined long
afterwards to be written down in
grim earnest by a half-frenzied old

man, and printed, in cold blood, by an English gentleman.

The horrible description of Mrs. Irving's personal appearance, and the other stories of the same connection, are recognised by Mrs. Oliphant as in substance Mrs. Carlyle's; whilst the malicious account of Mrs. Basil Montague's head-dress is attributed by Carlyle himself to his wife. Still, after dividing the total, there is a good helping for each, and blame would justly be Carlyle's due if we did not remember, as we are bound to do, that, interesting as these three sketches are, their interest is pathological, and ought never to have been given us. Mr. Froude should have read them in tears, and burnt them in fire. There is nothing surprising in the state of mind which produced them. They are easily accounted for by our sorrow-laden experience. It is a familiar feeling which prompts

a man, suddenly bereft of one whom
he alone really knew and loved, to
turn in his fierce indignation upon
the world, and deride its idols whom
all are praising, and which yet to him
seem ugly by the side of one of whom
no one speaks. To be angry with
such a sentence as 'scribbling Sands
and Eliots, not fit to compare with
my incomparable Jeannie,' is at
once inhuman and ridiculous. This
is the language of the heart, not of
the head. It is no more criticism
than is the trumpeting of a wounded
elephant zoology.

Happy is the man who at such a
time holds both peace and pen ; but
unhappiest of all is he who, having
dipped his sorrow into ink, entrusts
the manuscript to a romantic historian.

The two volumes of the 'Life,' and
the three volumes of Mrs. Carlyle's
'Correspondence,' unfortunately did

not pour oil upon the troubled waters. The partizanship they evoked was positively indecent. Mrs. Carlyle had her troubles and her sorrows, as have most women who live under the same roof with a man of creative genius; but of one thing we may be quite sure, that she would have been the first, to use her own expressive language, to require God 'particularly to damn' her impertinent sympathizers. As for Mr. Froude, he may yet discover his Nemesis in the spirit of an angry woman whose privacy he has invaded, and whose diary he has most wantonly published.

These dark clouds are ephemeral. They will roll away, and we shall once more gladly recognise the lineaments of an essentially lofty character, of one who, though a man of genius and of letters, neither outraged society nor stooped to it; was

neither a rebel nor a slave ; who in
poverty scorned wealth; who never
mistook popularity for fame; but
from the first assumed, and throughout maintained, the proud attitude of
one whose duty it was to teach and
not to tickle mankind.

Brother-dunces, lend me your ears!
not to crop, but that I may whisper
into their furry depths : ' Do not
quarrel with genius. We have none
ourselves, and yet are so constituted
that we cannot live without it.'

ON THE ALLEGED OBSCU-RITY OF MR. BROWNING'S POETRY.

'THE sanity of true genius' was a happy phrase of Charles Lamb's. Our greatest poets were our sanest men. Chaucer, Spenser, Shakespeare, Milton, and Wordsworth might have defied even a mad doctor to prove his worst.

To extol sanity ought to be unnecessary in an age which boasts its realism; but yet it may be doubted whether, if the author of the phrase just quoted were to be allowed once more to visit the world he loved so well and left so reluctantly, and could be induced to forswear his Elizabethans and devote himself to the literature of the day, he would find many books which his fine critical faculty would allow him to pronounce 'healthy,' as he once pronounced 'John Buncle' to be in the presence of a Scotchman, who could not for the life of him understand how a book could properly be said to enjoy either good or bad health.

But, however this may be, this much is certain, that lucidity is one of the chief characteristics of sanity. A sane man ought not to be unintelligible.   Lucidity is good everywhere, for all time and in all things, in a letter, in a speech, in a book, in a poem.   Lucidity is not simplicity. A lucid poem is not necessarily an easy one.   A great poet may tax our brains, but he ought not to puzzle our wits.   We may often have to ask in Humility, What *does* he mean ? but not in despair, What *can* he mean ?

Dreamy and inconclusive the poet

sometimes, nay, often, cannot help being, for dreaminess and inconclu-siveness are conditions of thought when dwelling on the very subjects that most demand poetical treat-ment.

Misty, therefore, the poet has our kind permission sometimes to be; but muddy, never! A great poet, like a great peak, must sometimes be allowed to have his head in the clouds, and to disappoint us of the wide prospect we had hoped to gain; but the clouds which envelop him must be attracted to, and not made by him.

In a sentence, though the poet may give expression to what Wordsworth has called 'the heavy and the weary weight of all this unintelligible world,' we, the much-enduring public who have to read his poems, are entitled to demand that the unintelligibility of which we are made to feel the

weight, should be all of it the
world's, and none of it merely the
poet's.

We should not have ventured to
introduce our subject with such very
general and undeniable observations,
had not experience taught us that
the best way of introducing any subject is by a string of platitudes, delivered after an oracular fashion.
They arouse attention, without ex-
hausting it, and afford the pleasant
sensation of thinking, without any of
the trouble of thought. But, the
subject once introduced, it becomes
necessary to proceed with it.

In considering whether a poet is
intelligible and lucid, we ought not to
grope and grub about his work in
search of obscurities and oddities,
but should, in the first instance at
all events, attempt to regard his
whole scope and range; to form some
estimate, if we can, of his general

purport and effect, asking ourselves,
for this purpose, such questions as
these : How are we the better for
him ?   Has he quickened any passion, lightened any burden, purified
any taste ?   Does he play any real
part in our lives ?   When we are in
love, do we whisper him in our lady's
ear ?   When we sorrow, does he ease
our pain ?   Can he calm the strife of
mental conflict ?   Has he had anything to say, which wasn't twaddle,
on those subjects which, elude analysis
as they may, and defy demonstration
as they do, are yet alone of perennial
interest—

'On man, on nature, and on human life,'

on the pathos of our situation, looking back on to the irrevocable and
forward to the unknown ?   If a poet
has said, or done, or been any of these
things to an appreciable extent, to
charge him with obscurity is both
folly and ingratitude.

But the subject may be pursued further, and one may be called upon to investigate this charge with reference to particular books or poems. In Browning's case this fairly may be done ; and then another crop of questions arises, such as: What is the book about, *i.e.*, with what subject does it deal, and what method of dealing does it employ? Is it didactical, analytical, or purely narrative? Is it content to describe, or does it aspire to explain? In common fairness these questions must be asked and answered, before we heave our critical half-bricks at strange poets. One task is of necessity more difficult than another. Students of geometry, who have pushed their researches into that fascinating science so far as the fifth proposition of the first book, commonly called the *Pons Asinorum* (though now that so many ladies read Euclid, it ought, in common justice to them, to be at least sometimes called the *Pons Asinarum*), will agree that though it may be more difficult to prove that the angles at the base of an isosceles triangle are equal, and that if the equal sides be produced, the angles on the other side of the base shall be equal, than it was to describe an equilateral triangle on a given finite straight line; yet no one but an ass would say that the fifth proposition was one whit less intelligible than the first. When we consider Mr. Browning in his later writings, it will be useful to bear this distinction in mind.

Our first duty, then, is to consider Mr. Browning in his whole scope and range, or, in a word, generally. This is a task of such dimensions and difficulty as, in the language of joint-stock prospectuses, 'to transcend individual enterprise,' and consequently, as we all know, a company has been

recently floated, or a society established, having Mr. Browning for its
principal object. It has a president,
two secretaries, male and female, and
a treasurer. You pay a guinea, and
you become a member. A suitable
reduction is, I believe, made in the un-
likely event of all the members of one
family flocking to be enrolled. The
existence of this society is a great
relief, for it enables us to deal with our
unwieldy theme in a light-hearted
manner, and to refer those who
have a passion for solid information
and profound philosophy to the
printed transactions of this learned
society, which, lest we should forget
all about it, we at once do.

When you are viewing a poet generally, as is our present plight, the first
question is : When was he born ?
The second, When did he (to use a
favourite phrase of the last century,
now in disuse)—When did he com-

...ence author? The third, How long
did he keep at it? The fourth, How
much has he written? And the fifth
may perhaps be best expressed in the
words of Southey's little Peterkin:

> ' "What good came of it all at last?"
> Quoth little Peterkin.'

Mr. Browning was born in 1812;
he commenced author with the frag-
ment called 'Pauline,' published in
1833. He is still writing, and his
works, as they stand upon my shelves
—for editions vary—number twenty-
three volumes. Little Peterkin's
question is not so easily answered;
but, postponing it for a moment, the
answers to the other four show that
we have to deal with a poet, more
than seventy years old, who has been
writing for half a century, and who
has filled twenty-three volumes. The
Browning Society at all events has
assets. The way I propose to deal
with this literary mass is to divide it

in two, taking the year 1864 as the line of cleavage. In that year the volume called 'Dramatis Personæ was published, and then nothing happened till the year 1868, when our poet presented the astonished English language with the four volumes and the 21,116 lines called 'The Ring and the Book,' a poem which it may be stated, for the benefit of that large, increasing, and highly interesting class of persons who prefer statistics to poetry, is longer than Pope's 'Homer's Iliad' by exactly 2,171 lines. We thus begin with 'Pauline' in 1833, and end with 'Dramatis Personæ' in 1864. We then begin again with the 'Ring and the Book,' in 1868; but when or where we shall end cannot be stated. 'Sordello,' published in 1840, is better treated apart, and is therefore excepted from the first period, to which chronologically it belongs.

Looking then at the first period, we find in its front eight plays :

1. ' Strafford,' written in 1836, when its author was twenty-four years old, and put upon the boards of Covent Garden Theatre on the 1st of May, 1837, Macready playing Strafford, and Miss Helen Faucit Lady Carlisle. It was received by all who saw it with enthusiasm ; but the Company, for reasons unconnected with the play, was rebellious ; and after running five nights, the man who played Pym threw up his part, and the theatre was closed.

2. ' Pippa Passes.'
3. ' King Victor and King Charles.
4. ' The Return of the Druses.'
5. ' A Blot in the 'Scutcheon.'

This beautiful and pathetic play was put on the stage of Drury Lane on the 11th of February, 1843, with Phelps as Lord Tresham, Miss Helen

5

Faucit as Mildred Tresham, and Mrs. Stirling, still known to us all, is Guendolen. It was a brilliant success. Mr. Browning was in the stage-box; and if it is any satisfaction for a poet to hear a crowded house cry 'Author, author!' that satisfaction has belonged to Mr. Browning. The play ran at Drury Lane till the 3rd of June 1843, and was subsequently revived by Mr. Phelps, during his 'memorable management' of Sadlers' Wells.

6. 'Colombe's Birthday.' Miss Helen Faucit put this upon the stage in 1852, when it was reckoned a success.

7. 'Luria.'

8. 'A Soul's Tragedy.'

To call any of these plays unintelligible is ridiculous; and nobody who has ever read them ever did, and why people who have not read them should

abuse them is hard to see. Were
society put upon its oath, we should
be surprised to find how many people
in high places have not read 'All's
Well that Ends Well,' or ' Timon of
Athens;' but they don't go about
saying these plays are unintelligible.
Like wise folk, they pretend to have
read them, and say nothing. In
Browning's case they are spared the
hypocrisy. No one need pretend to
have read ' A Soul's Tragedy;' and
it seems, therefore, inexcusable for
anyone to assert that one of the
plainest, most pointed, and piquant
bits of writing in the language is
unintelligible. But surely something
more may be truthfully said of these
plays than that they are comprehen-
sible. First of all, they are *plays*,
and not *works*—like the dropsical
dramas of Sir Henry Taylor and Mr.
Swinburne. Some of them have
stood the ordeal of actual represen-

tation ; and though it would be absurd to pretend that they met with
that overwhelming measure of success our critical age has reserved for
such dramatists as the late Lord
Lytton, the author of ' Money,' the
late Tom Taylor, the author of ' The
Overland Route,' the late Mr. Robert-
son, the author of ' Caste,' Mr. H.
Byron, the author of ' Our Boys,'
Mr. Wills, the author of ' Charles I.,'
Mr. Burnand, the author of ' The
Colonel,' and Mr. Gilbert, the author
of so much that is great and glori-
ous in our national drama ; at all
events they proved themselves able
to arrest and retain the attention of
very ordinary audiences. But who
can deny dignity and even grandeur
to ' Luria,' or withhold the meed
of a melodious tear from ' Mildred
Tresham'? What action of what
play is more happily conceived or
better rendered than that of ' Pippa

Passes'?—where innocence and its reverse, tender love and violent passion, are presented with emphasis, and yet blended into a dramatic unity and a poetic perfection, entitling the author to the very first place amongst those dramatists of the century who have laboured under the enormous disadvantage of being poets to start with.

Passing from the plays, we are next attracted by a number of splendid poems, on whose base the structure of Mr. Browning's fame perhaps rests most surely — his dramatic pieces—poems which give utterance to the thoughts and feelings of persons other than himself, or, as he puts it, when dedicating a number of them to his wife :

‘ Love, you saw me gather men and women,
Live or dead, or fashioned by my fancy,
Enter each and all, and use their service,
Speak from every mouth the speech—a poem ;'

or, again, in 'Sordello':

' By making speak, myself kept out of view
The very man, as he was wont to do.'

At a rough calculation, there must be at least sixty of these pieces. Let me run over the names of a very few of them. 'Saul,' a poem beloved by all true women; 'Caliban,' which the men, not unnaturally perhaps, often prefer. The 'Two Bishops'; the sixteenth century one ordering his tomb of jasper and basalt in St. Praxed's Church, and his nineteenth century successor rolling out his post-prandial *Apologia*. 'My Last Duchess,' the 'Soliloquy in a Spanish Cloister,' 'Andrea del Sarto,' 'Fra Lippo Lippi,' 'Rabbi Ben Ezra,' 'Cleon,' 'A Death in the Desert,' 'The Italian in England,' and 'The Englishman in Italy.'

It is plain truth to say that no other English poet, living or dead,

Shakespeare excepted, has so heaped up human interest for his readers as has Robert Browning.

Fancy stepping into a room and finding it full of Shakespeare's principal characters! What a babel of tongues! What a jostling of wits! How eagerly one's eye would go in search of Hamlet and Sir John Falstaff, but droop shudderingly at the thought of encountering the distraught gaze of Lady Macbeth! We should have no difficulty in recognising Beatrice in the central figure of that lively group of laughing courtiers; whilst did we seek Juliet, it would, of course, be by appointment on the balcony. To fancy yourself in such company is pleasant matter for a midsummer's night's dream. No poet has such a gallery as Shakespeare, but of our modern poets Browning comes nearest him.

Against these dramatic pieces the

charge of unintelligibility fails as
completely as it does against the
plays.   They are all perfectly intelligible ; but—and here is the rub—
they are not easy reading, like the
estimable writings of the late Mrs.
Hemans.   They require the same
honest attention as it is the fashion
to give to a lecture of Professor
Huxley's or a sermon of Canon
Liddon's: and this is just what too
many persons will not give to poetry.
They

> ' Love to hear
> A soft pulsation in their easy ear ;
> To turn the page, and let their senses drink
> A lay that shall not trouble them to think.'

It is no great wonder it should be
so.   After dinner, when disposed to
sleep, but afraid of spoiling our night's
rest, behold the witching hour reserved by the nineteenth century for
the study of poetry !   This treatment
of the muse deserves to be held up to
everlasting scorn and infamy in a

passage of Miltonic strength and
splendour. We, alas! must be content with the observation, that such
an opinion of the true place of poetry
in the life of a man excites, in the
breasts of the rightminded, feelings
akin to those which Charles Lamb
ascribes to the immortal Sarah Battle,
when a young gentleman of a literary
turn, on taking a hand in her favourite
game of whist, declared that he saw
no harm in unbending the mind, now
and then, after serious studies, in re-
creations of that kind. She could
not bear, so Elia proceeds, 'to have
her noble occupation, to which she
wound up her faculties, considered in
that light. It was her business, her
duty—the thing she came into the
world to do—and she did it: she
unbent her mind, afterwards, over a
book!' And so the lover of poetry
and Browning, after winding-up his
faculties over 'Comus' or 'Para-

celsus,' over ' Julius Cæsar ' or ' Strafford,' may afterwards, if he is so
minded, unbend · himself over the
' Origin of Species,' or that still more
fascinating record which tells us how
little curly worms, only give them
time enough, will cover with earth
even the larger kind of stones.

Next to these dramatic pieces
come what we may be content to
call simply poems : some lyrical,
some narrative.   The latter are
straightforward enough, and, as a
rule, full of spirit and humour ; but
this is more than can always be said
of the lyrical pieces. Now, for the
first time, in dealing with this first
period, excluding ' Sordello,' we strike
difficulty. The Chinese puzzle comes
in.   We wonder whether it all turns
on the punctuation. And the awkward
thing for Mr. Browning's reputation
is this, that these bewildering poems
are, for the most part, very short.

We say awkward, for it is not more certain that Sarah Gamp liked her beer drawn mild, than it is that your Englishman likes his poetry cut short; and so, accordingly, it often happens that some estimable paterfamilias takes up an odd volume of Browning his volatile son or moonstruck daughter has left lying about, pishes and pshaws ! and then, with an air of much condescension and amazing candour, remarks that he will give the fellow another chance, and not condemn him unread. So saying, he opens the book, and carefully selects the very shortest poem he can find ; and in a moment, without sign or signal, note or warning, the unhappy man is floundering up to his neck in lines like these, which are the third and final stanza of a poem called ' Another Way of Love ' :

> ' And after, for pastime
> If June be refulgent

With flowers in completeness,
All petals, no prickles,
Delicious as trickles
Of wine poured at mass-time,
And choose One indulgent
To redness and sweetness ;
Or if with experience of man and of spider,
She use my June lightning, the strong insect-ridder
To stop the fresh spinning,—why June will con-
sider.'

He comes up gasping, and more
than ever persuaded that Browning's
poetry is a mass of inconglomerate
nonsense, which nobody understands
—least of all members of the Browning Society.

We need be at no pains to find a
meaning for everything Mr. Browning has written. But when all is
said and done—when these few freaks
of a crowded brain are thrown overboard to the sharks of verbal criticism
who feed on such things—Mr. Browning and his great poetical achievement remain behind to be dealt with
and accounted for. We do not get
rid of the Laureate by quoting :

'O darling room, my heart's delight
Dear room, the apple of my sight,
With thy two couches soft and white
There is no room so exquisite—
No little room so warm and bright
Wherein to read, wherein to write ;

or of Wordsworth by quoting :

' At this, my boy hung down his head :
He blushed with shame, nor made reply,
And five times to the child I said,
" Why, Edward ? tell me why ?" '—

or of Keats by remembering that he
once addressed a young lady as
follows :

'O come, Georgiana ! the rose is full blown,
The riches of Flora are lavishly strown :
The air is all softness and crystal the streams,
The west is resplendently clothed in beams.'

The strength of a rope may be but
the strength of its weakest part ; but
poets are to be judged in their happiest hours, and in their greatest works.

Taking, then, this first period of
Mr. Browning's poetry as a whole,
and asking ourselves if we are the
richer for it, how can there be any
doubt as to the reply ? What points
of human interest has he left un-

touched ?   With what phase of life,
character, or study does he fail to
sympathize ?   So far from being the
rough-hewn block 'dull fools' have
supposed him, he is the most dilet-
tante of great poets.   Do you dabble
in art and perambulate picture-gal-
leries ?   Browning must be your
favourite poet: he is art's historian.
Are you devoted to music ?   So is
he : and alone of our poets has sought
to fathom in verse the deep mysteries
of sound.   Do you find it impossible
to keep off theology ?   Browning has
more theology than most bishops—
could puzzle Gamaliel and delight
Aquinas.   Are you in love ?   Read
 A Last Ride Together,' 'Youth and
Art,' 'A Portrait,' 'Christine,' 'In a
Gondola,' 'By the Fireside,' 'Love
amongst the Ruins,' 'Time's Re-
venges,' 'The Worst of It,' and a
lost of others, being careful always
to end with 'A Madhouse Cell'; and
we are much mistaken if you do not

put Browning at the very head and
front of the interpreters of passion.
The many moods of sorrow are reflected in his verse, whilst mirth,
movement, and a rollicking humour
abound everywhere.

I will venture upon but three quotations, for it is late in the day to be
quoting Browning. The first shall
be a well-known bit of blank verse
about art from ' Fra Lippo Lippi':

' For, don't you mark, we're made so that we love
  First when we see them painted, things we have
    passed
  Perhaps a hundred times, nor cared to see :
  And so they are better painted—better to us,
  Which is the same thing. Art was given for
    that—
  God uses us to help each other so,
  Lending our minds out. Have you noticed now
  Your cullion's hanging face ? A bit of chalk,
  And, trust me, but you should though. Ho'
    much more
  If I drew higher things with the same truth !
  That were to take the prior's pulpit-place—
  Interpret God to all of you ! Oh, oh !
  It makes me mad to see what men shall do,
  And we in our graves ! This world's no blot for
    us,
  Nor blank : it means intensely, and means good.
  To find its meaning is my meat and drink.'

The second is some rhymed rhetoric
from ' Holy Cross Day '—the testimony of the dying Jew in Rome:

> ' This world has been harsh and strange,
> Something is wrong : there needeth a change.
> But what or where ? at the last or first ?
> In one point only we sinned at worst.

> ' The Lord will have mercy on Jacob yet,
> And again in his border see Israel set.
> When Judah beholds Jerusalem,
> The stranger seed shall be joined to them :
> To Jacob's house shall the Gentiles cleave :
> So the prophet saith, and his sons believe.

> ' Ay, the children of the chosen race
> Shall carry and bring them to their place ;
> In the land of the Lord shall lead the same,
> Bondsmen and handmaids.   Who shall blame
> When the slaves enslave, the oppressed ones o'er
> The oppressor triumph for evermore ?

> ' God spoke, and gave us the word to keep :
> Bade never fold the hands, nor sleep
> 'Mid a faithless world, at watch and ward,
> Till the Christ at the end relieve our guard.
> By His servant Moses the watch was set :
> Though near upon cockcrow, we keep it yet.

> Thou ! if Thou wast He, who at mid-watch came,
> By the starlight naming a dubious Name ;
> And if we were too heavy with sleep, too rash
> With fear—O Thou, if that martyr-gash
> Fell on Thee, coming to take Thine own,
> And we gave the Cross, when we owed the
>   throne ;

'Thou art the Judge. We are bruised thus.
But, the Judgment over, join sides with us !
Thine, too, is the cause ! and not more Thine
Than ours is the work of these dogs and swine,
Whose life laughs through and spits at their creed,
Who maintain Thee in word, and defy Thee in
deed.

'We withstood Christ then ? Be mindful how
At least we withstand Barabbas now !
Was our outrage sore ? But the worst we spared
To have called these—Christians—had we dared
Let defiance to them pay mistrust of Thee,
And Rome make amends for Calvary !

By the torture, prolonged from age to age ;
By the infamy, Israel's heritage ;
By the Ghetto's plague, by the garb's disgrace,
By the badge of shame, by the felon's place,
By the branding-tool, the bloody whip,
And the summons to Christian fellowship,

We boast our proof, that at least the Jew
Would wrest Christ's name from the devil's crew.

The last quotation shall be from
the veritable Browning—of one of
those poetical audacities none ever
dared but the Danton of modern
poetry. Audacious in its familiar
realism, in its total disregard of
poetical environment, in its rugged
abruptness : but supremely successful, and alive with emotion :

6

' What is he buzzing in my ears ?
   Now that I come to die,
Do I view the world as a vale of tears ?
   Ah, reverend sir, not I.

' What I viewed there once, what I view again,
   Where the physic bottles stand
On the table's edge, is a suburb lane,
   With a wall to my bedside hand.

' That lane sloped, much as the bottles do,
   From a house you could descry
O'er the garden-wall.   Is the curtain blue
   Or green to a healthy eye ?

To mine, it serves for the old June weather,
   Blue above lane and wall ;
And that farthest bottle, labelled " Ether,"
   Is the house o'ertopping all.

At a terrace somewhat near its stopper,
   There watched for me, one June,
A girl—I know, sir, it's improper :
   My poor mind's out of tune.

' Only there was a way—you crept
   Close by the side, to dodge
Eyes in the house—two eyes except.
   They styled their house " The Lodge."

' What right had a lounger up their lane ?
   But by creeping very close,
With the good wall's help their eyes might strain
   And stretch themselves to oes,

Yet never catch her and me together,
   As she left the attic—there,
By the rim of the bottle labelled " Ether "—
   And stole from stair to stair,

'And stood by the rose-wreathed gate. Alas !
 We loved, sir ; used to meet.
How sad and bad and mad it was !
 But then, how it was sweet !'

The second period of Mr. Browning's poetry demands a different line
of argument ; for it is, in my judgment, folly to deny that he has of
late years written a great deal which
makes very difficult reading indeed.
No doubt you may meet people who
tell you that they read the 'Ring
and the Book' for the first time
without much mental effort ; but you
will do well not to believe them.
These poems are difficult—they cannot help being so. What is the
'Ring and the Book'? A huge novel
in 20,000 lines—told after the method
not of Scott but of Balzac ; it tears
the hearts out of a dozen characters ;
it tells the same story from ten different points of view. It is loaded
with detail of every kind and description : you are let off nothing. As

6—2

with a schoolboy's life at a large
school, if he is to enjoy it at all, he
must fling himself into it, and care
intensely about everything—so the
reader of the ' Ring and the Book'
must be interested in everybody and
everything, down to the fact that the
eldest daughter of the counsel for the
prosecution of Guido is eight years
old on the very day he is writing
his speech, and that he is going to
have fried liver and parsley for his
supper.

If you are prepared for this, you
will have your reward; for the *style*,
though rugged and involved, is
throughout, with the exception of
the speeches of counsel, eloquent,
and at times superb; and as for
the *matter*, if your interest in human
nature is keen, curious, almost professional—if nothing man, woman,
or child has been, done, or suffered,
or conceivably can be, do, or suffer,

is without interest for you; if you
are fond of analysis, and do not
shrink from dissection — you will
prize the 'Ring and the Book' as
the surgeon prizes the last great con-
tribution to comparative anatomy or
pathology.

But this sort of work tells upon
style. Browning has, I think, fared
better than some writers. To me, at
all events, the step from 'A Blot in
the 'Scutcheon' to the 'Ring and
the Book' is not so marked as is
the *mauvais pas* that lies between
'Amos Barton' and 'Daniel De-
ronda.' But difficulty is not obscurity. One task is more difficult
than another. The angles at the
base of the isosceles triangles are apt
to get mixed, and to confuse us all
—man and woman alike. 'Prince
Hohenstiel' something or another is
a very difficult poem, not only to
pronounce but to read; but if a poet

chooses as his subject Napoleon III.
—in whom the cad, the coward, the
idealist, and the sensualist were in-
extricably mixed—and purports to
make him unbosom himself over a
bottle of Gladstone claret in a tavern
in Leicester Square, you cannot expect that the product should belong
to the same class of poetry as Mr.
Coventry Patmore's admirable 'Angel
in the House.'

It is the method that is difficult.
Take the husband in the ' Ring and
the Book.' Mr. Browning remorse-
lessly hunts him down, tracks him to
the last recesses of his mind, and
there bids him stand and deliver.
He describes love, not only broken
but breaking; hate in its germ;
doubt at its birth. These are difficult things to do either in poetry or
prose, and people with easy, flowing
Addisonian or Tennysonian styles
cannot do them.

I seem to overhear a still, small voice asking, But are they worth doing ? or at all events is it the pro· vince of art to do them ? The ques· tion ought not to be asked. It is heretical, being contrary to the whole direction of the latter half of this century. The chains binding us to the rocks of realism are faster riveted every day ; and the Perseus who is destined to cut them is, I expect, some mischievous little boy at a Board-school. But as the question has been asked, I will own that some- times, even when deepest in works of. this, the now orthodox school, I have been harassed by distressing doubts whether, after all, this enormous labour is not in vain ; and, wearied by the effort, overloaded by the detail, bewildered by the argument, and sickened by the pitiless dissection of character and motive, have been tempted to cry aloud, quoting—or rather, in the agony of the moment, misquoting—Coleridge:

'Simplicity—
Thou better name than all the family of Fame.'

But this ebullition of feeling is childish and even sinful. We must take our poets as we do our meals—as they are served up to us. Indeed, you may, if full of courage, give a cook notice, but not the time-spirit who makes our poets. We may be sure—to appropriate an idea of the late Sir James Stephen—that if Robert Browning had lived in the sixteenth century, he would not have written a poem like the 'Ring and the Book'; and if Edmund Spenser had lived in the nineteenth century he would not have written a poem like the 'Faerie Queen.'

It is therefore idle to arraign Mr. Browning's later method and style for possessing difficulties and intricacies which are inherent to it. The

method, at all events, has an interest
of its own, a strength of its own, a
grandeur of its own. If you do not
like it, you must leave it alone. You
are fond, you say, of romantic poetry;
well, then, take down your Spenser
and qualify yourself to join 'the small
transfigured band' of those who are
able to take their Bible-oaths they
have read their 'Faerie Queen' all
through. The company, though small
is delightful, and you will have plenty
to talk about without abusing Browning, who probably knows his Spenser
better than you do. Realism will
not for ever dominate the world of
letters and art — the fashion of all
things passeth away—but it has already earned a great place: it has
written books, composed poems,
painted pictures, all stamped with
that 'greatness' which, despite fluc-
tuations, nay, even reversals of taste
and opinion. means immortality.

But against Mr. Browning's later poems it is sometimes alleged that their meaning is obscure because their grammar is bad. A cynic was once heard to observe with reference to that noble poem 'The Grammarian's Funeral,' that it was a pity the talented author had ever since allowed himself to remain under the delusion that he had not only buried the grammarian, but his grammar also. It is doubtless true that Mr. Browning has some provoking ways, and is something too much of a verbal acrobat. Also, as his witty parodist, the pet poet of six generations of Cambridge undergraduates, reminds us :

'He loves to dock the smaller parts of speech,
    As we curtail the already curtailed cur.'

It is perhaps permissible to weary a little of his *i*'s and *o*'s, but we believe we cannot be corrected when we say that Browning is a poet whose

grammar will bear scholastic investi-
gation better than that of most of
Apollo's children.

A word about 'Sordello.' One half
of 'Sordello,' and that, with Mr.
Browning's usual ill-luck, the first
half, is undoubtedly obscure. It is
as difficult to read as 'Endymion'
or the 'Revolt of Islam,' and for the
same reason—the author's lack of
experience in the art of composition.
We have all heard of the young
architect who forgot to put a staircase in his house, which contained
fine rooms, but no way of getting
into them. 'Sordello' is a poem
without a staircase. The author, still
in his twenties, essayed a high thing.
For his subject—

> 'He singled out
> Sordello compassed murkily about
> With ravage of six long sad hundred years.'

He partially failed; and the British
public, with its accustomed gene-

rosity, and in order, I suppose, to encourage the others, has never ceased girding at him, because forty-two years ago he published, at his own charges, a little book of two hundred and fifty pages, which even such of them as were then able to read could not understand.

Poetry should be vital — either stirring our blood by its divine movement, or snatching our breath by its divine perfection. To do both is supreme glory; to do either is enduring fame.

There is a great deal of beautiful poetical writing to be had nowadays from the booksellers. It is interesting reading, but as one reads one trembles. It smells of mortality. It would seem as if, at the very birth of most of our modern poems,

> 'The conscious Parcæ threw
> Upon their roseate lips a Stygian hue.'

That their lives may be prolonged is

my pious prayer. In these bad days, when it is thought more education- ally useful to know the principle of the common pump than Keats's 'Ode on a Grecian Urn,' one canno afford to let any good poetry die.

But when we take down Browning, we cannot think of him and the 'wormy bed' together. He is so un- mistakably and deliciously alive. Die, indeed! when one recalls the ideal characters he has invested with reality; how he has described love and joy, pain and sorrow, art and music; as poems like 'Childe Roland, 'Abt Vogler,' 'Evelyn Hope,' 'The Worst of It,' 'Pictor Ignotus,' 'The Lost Leader,' 'Home Thoughts from Abroad,' 'Old Pictures in Florence,' 'Herve Riel,' 'A Householder,' 'Fears and Scruples,' come tumbling into one's memory, one over another—we are tempted to employ the language of hyperbole, and to answer the

question ' Will Browning die ?' by exclaiming, 'Yes; when Niagara stops.
In him indeed we can

> ' Discern
> Infinite passion and the pain
> Of finite hearts that yearn.'

But love of Mr. Browning's poetry
is no exclusive cult.

Of Lord Tennyson it is needless
to speak.   Even forty years of popularity and mimicry cannot rob his
verse of distinction.

Mr. Arnold may have a limited
poetical range and a restricted style,
but within that range and in that
style, surely we must exclaim :

> ' Whence that completed form of all completeness ?
> Whence came that high perfection of all sweet-
>   ness ?'

Rossetti's luscious lines seldom fail
to cast a spell by which

> ' In sundry moods 'tis pastime to be bound.'

William Morris has a sunny slope
of Parnassus all to himself, and Mr.
Swinburne has written some verses

over which the world will long love to linger.

Dull must he be of soul who can take up Cardinal Newman's ' Verses on Various Occasions,' or Miss Christina Rossetti's poems, and lay them down without recognising their diverse charm.

Let us be Catholics in this great matter, and burn our candles at many shrines. In the pleasant realms of poesy, no liveries are worn, no paths prescribed ; you may wander where you will, stop where you like, and worship whom you love. Nothing is demanded of you, save this, that in all your wanderings and worships, you keep two objects steadily in view—two, and two only, truth and beauty.

TRUTH-HUNTING.

IT is common knowledge that the distinguishing characteristic of the day is the zeal displayed by us all in hunting after Truth. A really not inconsiderable portion of whatever time we are able to spare from making or losing money or reputation, is devoted to this sport, whilst both reading and conversation are largely impressed into the same service.

Nor are there wanting those who avow themselves anxious to see this, their favourite pursuit, raised to the dignity of a national institution. They would have Truth-hunting established and endowed.

Mr. Carlyle has somewhere described with great humour the 'dreadfully painful' manner in which Kepler made his celebrated calculations and discoveries; but our young men of talent fail to see the joke, and take no pleasure in such anecdotes. Truth, they feel, is not to be had from them on any such terms. And why should it be? Is it not notorious that all who are lucky enough to supply wants grow rapidly and enormously rich; and is not Truth a now recognised want in ten thousand homes—wherever, indeed, persons are to be found wealthy enough to pay Mr. Mudie a guinea and so far literate as to be able to read? What, save the modesty, is there surprising in the demand now made on behalf of some young people, whose means are incommensurate with their talents, that they should be allowed, as a reward for doling out monthly or quarterly portions of truth, to live in houses rent-free, have their meals for nothing, and a trifle of money besides? Would Bass consent to supply us with beer in return for board and lodging, we of course defraying the actual cost of his brewery, and allowing him some £300 a year for himself? Who, as he read about 'Sun-spots,' or 'Fresh Facts for Darwin,' or the 'True History of Modesty or Veracity,' showing how it came about that these high-sounding virtues are held in their present somewhat general esteem, would find it in his heart to grudge the admirable authors their freedom from petty cares?

But, whether Truth - hunting be ever established or not, no one can doubt that it is a most fashionable pastime, and one which is being pursued with great vigour.

All hunting is so far alike as to

lead one to believe that there must sometimes occur in Truth-hunting, just as much as in fox-hunting, long pauses, whilst the covers are being drawn in search of the game, and when thoughts are free to range at will in pursuit of far other objects than those giving their name to the sport. If it should chance to any Truth-hunter, during some 'lull in his hot chase,' whilst, for example, he is waiting for the second volume of an 'Analysis of Religion,' or for the last thing out on the Fourth Gospel, to take up this book, and open it at this page, we should like to press him for an answer to the following question: 'Are you sure that it is a good thing for you to spend so much time in speculating about matters outside your daily life and walk?'

Curiosity is no doubt an excellent quality. In a critic it is especially

excellent. To want to know all
about a thing, and not merely one
man's account or version of it; to
see all round it, or, at any rate, as
far round as is possible; not to be
lazy or indifferent, or easily put off,
or scared away—all this is really
very excellent. Sir Fitz James Stephen
professes great regret that we have
not got Pilate's account of the events
immediately preceding the Cruci-
fixion. He thinks it would throw
great light upon the subject; and
no doubt, if it had occurred to the
Evangelists to adopt in their narra-
tives the method which long afterwards recommended itself to the
author of 'The Ring and the Book,'
we should now be in possession of a
mass of very curious information.
But, excellent as all this is in the
realm of criticism, the question remains, How does a restless habit of
mind tell upon conduct?

John Mill was not one from whose lips the advice '*Stare super antiquas vias*' was often heard to proceed, and he was by profession a speculator, yet in that significant book, the 'Autobiography,' he describes this age of Truth-hunters as one 'of weak convictions, paralyzed intellects, and growing laxity of opinions.'

Is Truth-hunting one of those active mental habits which, as Bishop Butler tells us, intensify their effects by constant use ; and are weak convictions, paralyzed intellects, and laxity of opinions amongst the effects of Truth-hunting on the majority of minds ? These are not unimportant questions.

Let us consider briefly the probable effects of speculative habits on conduct.

The discussion of a question of conduct has the great charm of justifying, if indeed not requiring, per-

sonal illustration; and this particular question is well illustrated by in-
stituting a comparison between the
life and character of Charles Lamb
and those of some of his distinguished friends.

Personal illustration, especially
when it proceeds by way of comparison, is always dangerous, and
the dangers are doubled when the
subjects illustrated and compared
are favourite authors. It behoves
us to proceed warily in this matter.
A dispute as to the respective merits
of Gray and Collins has been known
to result in a visit to an attorney
and the revocation of a will. An
avowed inability to see anything in
Miss Austen's novels is reported to
have proved destructive of an otherwise good chance of an Indian judge-
ship. I believe, however, I run no
great risk in asserting that, of all
English authors, Charles Lamb is

the one loved most warmly and emo-
tionally by his admirers, amongst
whom I reckon only those who are
as familiar with the four volumes
of his 'Life and Letters' as with
' Elia.'

But how does he illustrate the
particular question now engaging
our attention ?

Speaking of his sister Mary, who,
as everyone knows, throughout
'Elia' is called his Cousin Bridget,
he says :

' It has been the lot of my cousin,
' oftener, perhaps, than I could have
' wished, to have had for her asso-
' ciates and mine freethinkers, leaders
and disciples of novel philosophies
'and systems, but she neither
' wrangles with nor accepts their
' opinions.'

Nor did her brother. He lived
his life cracking his little jokes and
reading his great folios, neither

wrangling with nor accepting the opinions of the friends he loved to see around him. To a contemporary stranger it might well have appeared as if his life were a frivolous and useless one as compared with those of these philosophers and thinkers. *They* discussed their great schemes and affected to probe deep mysteries, and were constantly asking, 'What is Truth ?' *He* sipped his glass, shuffled his cards, and was content with the humbler inquiry, 'What are Trumps ?' But to us, looking back upon that little group, and knowing what we now do about each member of it, no such mistake is possible. To us it is plain beyond all question that, judged by whatever standard of excellence it is possible for any reasonable human being to take, Lamb stands head and shoulders a better man than any of them. No need to stop to compare him with

Godwin, or Hazlitt, or Lloyd; let us
boldly put him in the scales with one
whose fame is in all the churches
—with Samuel Taylor Coleridge,
'logician, metaphysician, bard.'

There are some men whom to
abuse is pleasant. Coleridge is not
one of them. How gladly we would
love the author of 'Christabel' if we
could! But the thing is flatly im
possible. His was an unlovely character. The sentence passed upon
him by Mr. Matthew Arnold (paren-
thetically, in one of the 'Essays in
Criticism') — 'Coleridge had no
morals '—is no less just than pitiless.
As we gather information about him
from numerous quarters, we find it
impossible to resist the conclusion
that he was a man neglectful of re-
straint, irresponsive to the claims of
those who had every claim upon him,
willing to receive, slow to give.

In early manhood Coleridge planned

a Pantisocracy where all the virtues were to thrive. Lamb did some-thing far more difficult: he played cribbage every night with his imbe-cile father, whose constant stream of querulous talk and fault-finding might well have goaded a far stronger man into practising and justifying neg-lect.

That Lamb, with all his admira-tion for Coleridge, was well aware of dangerous tendencies in his character, is made apparent by many letters, notably by one written in 1796, in which he says :

' O my friend, cultivate the filial
' feelings ! and let no man think him-
' self released from the kind charities
' of relationship : these shall give him
' peace at the last ; these are the best
' foundation for every species of bene-
' volence. I rejoice to hear that you
' are reconciled with all your rela-
' tions.'

This surely is as valuable an 'aid to reflection' as any supplied by the Highgate seer.

Lamb gave but little thought to the wonderful difference between the ' reason ' and the ' understanding.' He preferred old plays—an odd diet, some may think, on which to feed the virtues; but, however that may be, the noble fact remains, that he, poor, frail boy! (for he was no more, when trouble first assailed him) stooped down and, without sigh or sign, took upon his own shoulders the whole burden of a life-long sorrow.

Coleridge married. Lamb, at the bidding of duty, remained single, wedding himself to the sad fortunes of his father and sister. Shall we pity him? No; he had his reward—the surpassing reward that is only within the power of literature to bestow. It was Lamb, and not

Coleridge, who wrote ' Dream-Child-
ren : a Reverie ':

' Then I told how for seven long
' years, in hope sometimes, some-
' times in despair, yet persisting ever,
' I courted the fair Alice W——n :
' and as much as children could under-
' stand, I explained to them what
' coyness and difficulty and denial
' meant in maidens—when, suddenly
' turning to Alice, the soul of the first
' Alice looked out at her eyes with
' such a reality of representment that
' I became in doubt which of them
' stood before me, or whose that
' bright hair was ; and while I stood
' gazing, both the children gradually
' grew fainter to my view, receding
' and still receding, till nothing at
' last but two mournful features were
' seen in the uttermost distance, which,
' without speech, strangely impressed
' upon me the effects of speech. " We
' are not of Alice nor of thee, nor are

' we children at all. The children of
' Alice call Bartrum father. We are
' nothing, less than nothing, and
' dreams. We are only *what might*
' *have been.*" '

Godwin ! Hazlitt ! Coleridge !
Where now are their ' novel philosophies and systems ' ? Bottled
moonshine, which does *not* improve
by keeping.

> ' Only the actions of the just
> Smell sweet and blossom in the dust.'

Were we disposed to admit that
Lamb would in all probability have
been as good a man as everyone
agrees he was—as kind to his father,
as full of self-sacrifice for the sake of
his sister, as loving and ready a friend
—even though he had paid more
heed to current speculations, it is
yet not without use in a time like
this, when so much stress is laid
upon anxious inquiry into the mys
teries of soul and body, to point out

how this man attained to a moral
excellence denied to his speculative
contemporaries ; performed duties
from which they, good men as they
were, would one and all have shrunk ;
how, in short, he contrived to achieve
what no one of his friends, not
even the immaculate Wordsworth or
the precise Southey, achieved—the
living of a life, the records of which
are inspiriting to read, and are indeed 'the presence of a good dif-
fused ;' and managed to do it all
without either 'wrangling with or
accepting' the opinions that 'hurtled
in the air' about him.

But *was* there no relation between
his unspeculative habit of mind and
his honest, unwavering service of
duty, whose voice he ever obeyed as
the ship the rudder ?   It would be
difficult to name anyone more unlike
Lamb, in many aspects of character,
than Dr. Johnson, for whom he had

(mistakenly) no warm regard; but they closely resemble one another in their indifference to mere speculation about things—if things they can be called—outside our human walk; in their hearty love of honest earthly life, in their devotion to their friends, their kindness to dependents, and in their obedience to duty. What caused each of them the most pain was the recollection of a past unkindness. The poignancy of Dr. Johnson's grief on one such recollection is historical; and amongst Lamb's letters are to be found several in which, with vast depths of feeling, he bitterly upbraids himself for neglect of old friends.

Nothing so much tends to blur moral distinctions, and to obliterate plain duties, as the free indulgence of speculative habits. We must all know many a sorry scrub who has fairly talked himself into the belief

that nothing but his intellectual difficulties prevents him from being another St. Francis. We think we
could suggest a few score of other
obstacles.

Would it not be better for most
people, if, instead of stuffing their
heads with controversy, they were
to devote their scanty leisure to
reading books, such as, to name
one only, Kaye's 'History of the
Sepoy War,' which are crammed
full of activities and heroisms, and
which force upon the reader's mind
the healthy conviction that, after
all, whatever mysteries may ap-
pertain to mind and matter, and
notwithstanding grave doubts as
to the authenticity of the Fourth
Gospel, it is bravery, truth and
honour, loyalty and hard work, each
man at his post, which make this
planet inhabitable ?

In these days of champagne and

shoddy, of display of teacups and
rotten foundations—especially, too,
now that the 'nexus' of 'cash pay-
ment,' which was to bind man to man
in the bonds of a common pecuniary
interest, is hopelessly broken—it becomes plain that the real wants of
the age are not analyses of religious
belief, nor discussions as to whether
' Person ' or ' Stream of Tendency '
are the apter words to describe God
by ; but a steady supply of honest,
plain-sailing men who can be safely
trusted with small sums, and to do
what in them lies to maintain the
honour of the various professions,
and to restore the credit of English
workmanship. We want Lambs,
not Coleridges. The verdict to be
striven for is not ' Well guessed,'
but ' Well done.'

All our remarks are confined to
the realm of opinion. Faith may
be well left alone, for she is, to give

8

her her due, our largest manufacturer of good works, and whenever her furnaces are blown out, morality suffers.

But speculation has nothing to do with faith. The region of speculation is the region of opinion, and a hazy, lazy, delightful region it is; good to talk in, good to smoke in, peopled with pleasant fancies and charming ideas, strange analogies and killing jests. How quickly the time passes there! how well it seems spent! The Philistines are all outside; everyone is reasonable and tolerant, and good-tempered; you think and scheme and talk, and look at everything in a hundred ways and from all possible points of view; and it is not till the company breaks up and the lights are blown out, and you are left alone with silence, that the doubt occurs to you, What is the good of it all?

Where is the actuary who can appraise the value of a man's opinions ? 'When we speak of a man's 'opinions,' says Dr. Newman, 'what 'do we mean but the collection of 'notions he happens to have ?' Hap-. pens to have ! How did he come by them ? It is the knowledge we all possess of the sorts of ways in which men get their opinions that makes us so little affected in our own minds by those of men for whose characters and intellects we may have great admiration. A sturdy Nonconformist minister, who thinks Mr. Gladstone the ablest and most honest man, as well as the ripest scholar within the three kingdoms, is no whit shaken in his Nonconformity by knowing that his idol has written in defence of the Apostolical Succession, and believes in special sacramental graces. Mr. Gladstone may have been a great student of Church history,

8—2

whilst Nonconformist reading under that head usually begins with Luther's Theses—but what of that? Is it not all explained by the fact that Mr. Gladstone was at Oxford in 1831? So at least the Nonconformist minister will think.

The admission frankly made, that these remarks are confined to the realms of opinion, prevents me from urging on everyone my prescription, but, with the two exceptions to be immediately named, I believe it would be found generally useful. It may be made up thus: 'As much 'reticence as is consistent with good-'breeding upon, and a wisely tempered indifference to, the various 'speculative questions now agitated 'in our midst.'

This prescription would be found to liberate the mind from all kinds of cloudy vapours which obscure the mental vision and conceal from men their real position, and would also set free a great deal of time which might be profitably spent in quite other directions.

The first of the two exceptions I have alluded to is of those who possess—whether honestly come by or not we cannot stop to inquire—strong convictions upon these very questions. These convictions they must be allowed to iterate and re-iterate, and to proclaim that in them is to be found the secret of all this (otherwise) unintelligible world.

The second exception is of those who pursue Truth as by a divine compulsion, and who can be likened only to the nympholepts of old; those unfortunates who, whilst carelessly strolling amidst sylvan shades, caught a hasty glimpse of the flowing robes or even of the gracious countenance of some spiritual inmate of the woods, in whose pursuit their whole lives were ever afterwards fruitlessly spent.

The nympholepts of Truth are profoundly interesting figures in the world's history, but their lives are melancholy reading, and seldom fail to raise a crop of gloomy thoughts. Their finely. touched spirits are not indeed liable to succumb to the ordinary temptations of life, and they thus escape the evils which usually follow in the wake of speculation ; but what is their labour's reward ?

Readers of Dr. Newman will remember, and will thank me for recalling it to mind, an exquisite passage, too long to be quoted, in which, speaking as a Catholic to his late Anglican associates, he reminds them how he once participated in their pleasures and shared their hopes, and thus concludes :

' When, too, shall I not feel the ' soothing recollection of those dear

' years which I spent in retirement,
' in preparation for my deliverance
' from Egypt, asking for light, and
' by degrees getting it, with less of
' temptation in my heart and sin on
' my conscience than ever before ?'

But the passage is sad as well
as exquisite, showing to us, as it
does, one who from his earliest
days has rejoiced in a faith in
God, intense, unwavering, constant;
harassed by distressing doubts, he
carries them all, in the devotion of
his faith, the warmth of his heart,
and the purity of his life, to the
throne where Truth sits in state;
living, he tells us, in retirement,
and spending great portions of every
day on his knees; and yet—we ask
the question with all reverence—what
did Dr. Newman get in exchange for
his prayers?

' I think it impossible to withstand
' the evidence which is brought for

'the liquefaction of the blood of St.
'Januarius at Naples, or for the mo-
'tion of the eyes of the pictures of
'the Madonna in the Roman States.
'I see no reason to doubt the ma-
'terial of the Lombard Cross at
'Monza, and I do not see why the
'Holy Coat at Trèves may not have
'been what it professes to be. I
'firmly believe that portions of the
'True Cross are at Rome and else-
'where, that the Crib of Bethlehem
'is at Rome, and the bodies of St.
'Peter and St. Paul; also I firmly
'believe that the relics of the Saints
'are doing innumerable miracles and
'graces daily. I firmly believe that
'before now Saints have raised the
'dead to life, crossed the seas with-
'out vessels, multiplied grain an⁻¹
'bread, cured incurable diseases, anc
'stopped the operations of the laws
'of the universe in a multitudè of
'ways.'

So writes Dr. Newman, with that candour, that passion for putting the case most strongly against himself, which is only one of the lovely characteristics of the man whose long life has been a miracle of beauty and grace, and who has contrived to instil into his very controversies more of the spirit of Christ than most men can find room for in their prayers. But the dilemma is an awkward one. Does the Madonna wink, or is Heaven deaf?

Oh, Spirit of Truth, where wert thou, when the remorseless deep of superstition closed over the head of John Henry Newman, who surely deserved to be thy best-loved son?

But this is a digression. With the nympholepts of Truth we have nought to do. They must be allowed to pursue their lonely and devious paths, and though the records of their wanderings, their conflicting conclusions, and their widely-parted resting-places may fill us with despair, still they are witnesses whose testimony we could ill afford to lose.

But there are not many nympholepts. The symptoms of the great majority of our modern Truth-hunters are very different, as they will, with their frank candour, be the first to admit. They are free 'to drop their swords and daggers' whenever so commanded, and it is high time they did.

With these two exceptions I think my prescription will be found of general utility, and likely to promote a healthy flow of good works.

I had intended to say something as to the effect of speculative habits upon the intellect, but cannot now do so. The following shrewd remark of Mr. Latham's in his interesting book on the 'Action of Examinations' may, however, be quoted;

its bearing will be at once seen, and
its truth recognised by many:

'A man who has been thus pro-
vided with views and acute obser-
' vations may have destroyed in him-
' self the germs of that power which
' he simulates. He might have had
' a thought or two now and then if
' he had been let alone, but if he is
' made first to aim at a standard of
' thought above his years, and then
' finds he can get the sort of thoughts
' he wants without thinking, he is in
' a fair way to be spoiled.

ACTORS.

MOST people, I suppose, at one time or another in their lives, have felt the charm of an actor's life, as they were free to fancy it, well-nigh irresistible.

What is it to be a great actor? I say a great actor, because (I am sure) no amateur ever fancied himself a small one. Is it not always to have the best parts in the best plays; to be the central figure of every group; to feel that attention is arrested the moment you come on the stage; and (more exquisite satisfaction still) to be aware that it is relaxed when you go off; to have silence secured for your smallest utterances; to know that the highest dramatic talent has

ACTORS. 125

been exercised to invent situations for the very purpose of giving effect to *your* words and dignity to *your* actions; to quell all opposition by the majesty of your bearing or the brilliancy of your wit; and finally, either to triumph over disaster, or if you be cast in tragedy, happier still, to die upon the stage, supremely pitied and honestly mourned for at least a minute? And then, from first to last, applause loud and long—not postponed, not even delayed, but following immediately after. For a piece of diseased egotism—that is, for a man—what a lot is this!

How pointed, how poignant the contrast between a hero on the boards and a hero in the streets! In the world's theatre the man who is really playing the leading part— did we but know it—is too often, in the general estimate, accounted but

one of the supernumeraries, a figure
in dingy attire, who might well be
spared, and who may consider himself well paid with a pound a week.
His utterances procure no silence.
He has to pronounce them as best
he may, whilst the gallery sucks its
orange, the pit pares its nails, the
boxes babble, and the stalls yawn.
Amidst these pleasant distractions
he is lucky if he is heard at all; and
perhaps the best thing that can befall
him is for somebody to think him
worth the trouble of a hiss. As for
applause, it may chance with such
men, if they live long enough, as it
has to the great ones who have pre-
ceded them, in their old age,

'When they are frozen up within, and quite
  The phantom of themselves,
To hear the world applaud the hollow ghost
  Which blamed the living man.'

The great actor may sink to sleep,
soothed by the memory of the tears

or laughter he has evoked, and wake to find the day far advanced, whose close is to witness the repetition of his triumph ; but the great man will lie tossing and turning as he reflects on the seemingly unequal war he is waging with stupidity and prejudice, and be tempted to exclaim, as Milton tells us he was, with the sad prophet Jeremy : ' Woe is me, my mother, that thou hast borne me, a man of strife and contention!'

The upshot of all this is, that it is a pleasanter thing to represent greatness than to be great.

But the actor's calling is not only pleasant in itself—it gives pleasure to others. In this respect, how favourably it contrasts with the three learned professions !

Few pleasures are greater than to witness some favourite character, which hitherto has been but vaguely bodied forth by our sluggish imagina-

tions, invested with all the graces
of living man or woman. A distinguished man of letters, who years
ago was wisely selfish enough to rob
the stage of a jewel and set it in his
own crown, has addressed to his wife
some radiant lines which are often
on my lips :

'Beloved, whose life is with mine own entwined,
  In whom, whilst yet thou wert my dream, I
    viewed,
Warm with the life of breathing womanhood,
What Shakespeare's visionary eye divined—
Pure Imogen ; high-hearted Rosalind,
Kindling with sunshine all the dusk greenwood ;
Or changing with the poet's changing mood,
Juliet, or Constance of the queenly mind.'

But a truce to these compliments.

'I come to bury Cæsar, not to praise him.'

It is idle to shirk disagreeable
questions, and the one I have to ask
is this, ' Has the world been wrong
in regarding with disfavour and lack
of esteem the great profession of the
stage ?

That the world, ancient and
modern, has despised the actor's

profession cannot be denied. An
affecting story I read many years
ago—in that elegant and entertaining
work, Lemprière's ' Classical Dic-
tionary '—well illustrates the feeling
of the Roman world. Julius Deci-
mus Laberius was a Roman knight
and dramatic author, famous for his
mimes, who had the misfortune to
irritate a greater Julius, the author
of the ' Commentaries,' when the
latter was at the height of his power.
Cæsar, casting about how best he
might humble his adversary, could
think of nothing better than to condemn him to take a leading part in
one of his own plays. Laberius en-
treated in vain. Cæsar was obdu
rate, and had his way. Laberius
played his part—how, Lemprière
sayeth not; but he also took his
revenge, after the most effectual of
all fashions, the literary. He composed and delivered a prologue of

9

considerable power, in which he records the act of spiteful tyranny, and
which, oddly enough, is the only
specimen of his dramatic art that
has come down to us. It contains
lines which, though they do not
seem to have made Cæsar, who sat
smirking in the stalls, blush for himself, make us, 1,900 years afterwards,
blush for Cæsar. The only lines,
however, now relevant are, being in-
terpreted, as follow :

'After having lived sixty years
'with honour, I left my home this
'morning a Roman knight, but I
'shall return to it this evening an
'infamous stage-player. Alas! I
'have lived a day too long.'

Turning to the modern world,
and to England, we find it here the
popular belief that actors are by
statute rogues, vagabonds, and sturdy
beggars. This, it is true, is founded
on a misapprehension of the effect

of 39 Eliz. chap. 4, which only pro-
vides that common players wandering
abroad without authority to play,
shall be taken to be 'rogues and
vagabonds;' a distinction which one
would have thought was capable of
being perceived even by the blunted
faculties of the lay mind.*

But the fact that the popular belief rests upon a misreading of an
Act of Parliament three hundred
years old does not affect the belief,
but only makes it exquisitely English, and as a consequence entirely
irrational.

Is there anything to be said in support of this once popular prejudice?

It may, I think, be supported by
two kinds of argument. One derived from the nature of the case,
the other from the testimony of
actors themselves.

A serious objection to an actor's

* See note at end of Essay.

calling is that from its nature it admits of no other test of failure or success than the contemporary opinion of the town. This in itself must go far to rob life of dignity. A Milton may remain majestically indifferent to the 'barbarous noise' of 'owls and cuckoos, asses, apes, and dogs,' but the actor can steel himself to no such fortitude. He can lodge no appeal to posterity. The owls must hoot, the cuckoos cry, the apes yell, and the dogs bark on his side, or he is undone. This is of course inevitable, but it is an unfortunate condition of an artist's life.

Again, no record of his art survives to tell his tale or account for his fame. When old gentlemen wax garrulous over actors dead and gone, young gentlemen grow somnolent. Chippendale the cabinet-maker is more potent than Garrick the actor.

The vivacity of the latter no longer charms (save in Boswell); the chairs of the former still render rest impossible in a hundred homes.

This, perhaps, is why no man of lofty genius or character has ever condescended to remain an actor. His lot pressed heavily even on so mercurial a trifler as David Garrick, who has given utterance to the feeling in lines as good perhaps as any ever written by a successful player:

' The painter's dead, yet still he charms the eye,
While England lives his fame shall never die ;
But he who struts his hour upon the stage
Can scarce protract his fame thro' half an age ;
Nor pen nor pencil can the actor save—
Both art and artist have one common grave.'

But the case must be carried farther than this, for the mere fact that a particular pursuit does not hold out any peculiar attractions for soaring spirits will not justify us in calling that pursuit bad names. I therefore proceed to say that the very act of acting, *i.e.*, the art of mimicry, or the representation of feigned emotions called up by sham situations, is, in itself, an occupation an educated man should be slow to adopt as the profession of a life.

I believe—for we should give the world as well as the devil its due— that it is to a feeling, a settled per· suasion of this sort, lying deeper than the surface brutalities and snobbishnesses visible to all, that we must attribute the contempt, seemingly so cruel and so ungrateful, the world has visited upon actors.

I am no great admirer of beards, be they never so luxuriant or glossy yet I own I cannot regard off the stage the closely shaven face of an actor without a feeling of pity, not akin to love. Here, so I cannot help saying to myself, is a man who has adopted a profession whose very first demand upon him is that he should destroy his own identity. It is not what you are, or what by study you may become, but how few obstacles you present to the getting of yourself up as somebody else, that settles the question of your fitness for the stage. Smoothness of face, mobility of feature, compass of voice—these things, but the toys of other trades, are the tools of this one.

Boswellians will remember the name of Tom Davies as one of frequent occurrence in the great biography. Tom was an actor of some repute, and (so it was said) read 'Paradise Lost' better than any man in England. One evening, when Johnson was lounging behind the scenes at Drury (it was, I hope before his pious resolution to go there no more), Davies made his appearance on his way to the stage in all the majesty and millinery of his part. The situation is pic-

turesque. The great and dingy
Reality of the eighteenth century,
the Immortal, and the bedizened
little player. 'Well, Tom,' said the
great man (and this is the whole
story), 'well, Tom, and what art
thou to-night?' 'What art thou
to-night?' It may sound rather like
a tract, but it will, I think, be found
difficult to find an answer to the
question consistent with any true
view of human dignity.

Our last argument derived from
the nature of the case is, that deli
berately to set yourself as the occupation of your life to amuse the
adult and to astonish, or even to
terrify, the infant population of your
native land, is to degrade yourself.

Three-fourths of the acted drama
is, and always must be, comedy,
farce, and burlesque. We are bored
to death by the huge inanities of
life. We observe with horror that

our interest in our dinner becomes languid. We consult our doctor, who simulates an interest in our stale symptoms, and after a little talk about Dr. Diet, Dr. Quiet, and Dr. Merriman, prescribes Toole. If we are very innocent we may in-quire what night we are to go, but if we do we are at once told that it doesn't in the least matter when we go, for it is always equally funny. Poor Toole! to be made up every night as a safe prescription for the blues! To make people laugh is not necessarily a crime, but to adopt as your trade the making people laugh by delivering for a hundred nights together another man's jokes, in a costume the author of the jokes would blush to be seen in, seems to me a somewhat unworthy proceed-ing on the part of a man of character and talent.

To amuse the British public is a

task of herculean difficulty and
danger, for the blatant monster is,
at times, as whimsical and coy as a
maiden, and if it once makes up its
mind not to be amused, nothing will
shake it.   The labour is enormous,
the sacrifice beyond what is demanded of saints.   And if you succeed, what is your reward ?   Read
the lives of comedians, and closing
them, you will see what good reason
an actor has for exclaiming with the
old-world poet :

   ' Odi profanum vulgus !'

We now turn to the testimony of
actors themselves.

   Shakespeare is, of course, my first
witness.   There is surely significance
in this.   'Others abide our question,'
begins Arnold's fine sonnet on Shakespeare—' others abide our question ;
thou art free.'   The little we know
about our greatest poet has become
a commonplace   It is a striking

tribute to the endless loquacity of man, and a proof how that great creature is not to be deprived of his talk, that he has managed to write quite as much about there being nothing to write about as he could have written about Shakespeare, if the author of 'Hamlet' had been as great an egoist as Rousseau. The fact, however, remains that he who has told us most about ourselves, whose genius has made the whole civilized world kin, has told us nothing about himself, except that he hated and despised the stage. To say that he has told us this is not, I think, any exaggeration. I have, of course, in mind the often quoted lines to be found in that sweet treasury of melodious verse and deep feeling, the 'Sonnets of Shakespeare.' The 110th begins thus:

' Alas ! 'tis true I have gone here and there,
And made myself a motley to the view,
Gor'd my own thoughts, sold cheap what is most
    dear,
Made old offences of affections new.'

And the 111th:

'O for my sake do thou with Fortune chide,
The guilty goddess of my harmful deeds,
That did not better for my life provide
Than public means, which public manners breeds.
Thence comes it that my name receives a brand,
And almost thence my nature is subdued
To what it works on, like the dyer's hand.
Pity me, then, and wish I were renewed.'

It is not much short of three centuries since those lines were written, but they seem still to bubble with a scorn which may indeed be called immortal.

'Sold cheap what is most dear.'

There, compressed in half a line, is the whole case against an actor's calling.

But it may be said Shakespeare was but a poor actor. He could write *Hamlet* and *As You Like It;* but when it came to casting the parts, the Ghost in the one and old Adam in the other were the best he could aspire to. Verbose biographers of Shakespeare, in their

dire extremity, and naturally desirous
of writing a big book about a big
man, have remarked at length that
it was highly creditable to Shakespeare that he was not, or at all
events that it does not appear that
he was, jealous, after the true thea-
trical tradition, of his more successful brethren of the buskin.

It surely might have occurred,
even to a verbose biographer in his
direst need, that to have had the wit
to write and actually to have written
the soliloquies in *Hamlet*, might con-
sole a man under heavier afflictions
than the knowledge that in the popular
estimate somebody else spouted those
soliloquies better than he did himself. I can as easily fancy Milton
jealous of Tom Davies as Shakespeare
of Richard Burbage. But — good,
bad, or indifferent—Shakespeare was
an actor, and as such I tender his
testimony

I now—for really this matter must be cut short—summon pell-mell all the actors and actresses who have ever strutted their little hour on the stage, and put to them the following comprehensive question: Is there in your midst one who had an honest, hearty, downright pride and pleasure in your calling, or do not you all (tell the truth) mournfully echo the lines of your great master (whom nevertheless you never really cared for), and with him

> 'Your fortunes chide,
> That did not better for your lives provide
> Than public means, which public manners breeds.'

They all assent: with wonderful unanimity.

But, seriously, I know of no recorded exception, unless it be Thomas Betterton, who held the stage for half a century—from 1661 to 1708—and who still lives, as much as an actor can, in the pages of

Colley Cibber's *Apology*. He was a
man apparently of simple character,
for he had only one benefit-night all
his life.

Who else is there? Read Macready's ' Memoirs '—the King Arthur
of the stage. You will find there, I
am sorry to say, all the actor's faults
—if faults they can be called which
seem rather hard necessities, the dis-
colouring of the dyer's hand; greedy
hungering after applause, endless
egotism, grudging praise—all are
there; not perhaps in the tropical
luxuriance they have attained elsewhere, but plain enough. But do we
not also find, deeply engrained and
constant, a sense of degradation, a
longing to escape from the stage for
ever?

He did not like his children to
come and see him act, and was
always regretting—heaven help him!
—that he wasn't a barrister-at-law

Look upon this picture and on that
Here we have Macbeth, that mighty
thane; Hamlet, the intellectual
symbol of the whole world of modern
thought; Strafford, in Robert Browning's fine play; splendid dresses,
crowded theatres, beautiful women,
royal audiences; and on the other
side, a rusty gown, a musty wig, a
fusty court, a deaf judge, an indifferent jury, a dispute about a bill of
lading, and ten guineas on your
brief—which you have not been paid,
and which you can't recover—why,
' 'tis Hyperion to a satyr !'

Again, we find Mrs. Siddons
writing of her sister's marriage :

'I have lost one of the sweetest
'companions in the world. She has
'married a respectable man, though
'of small fortune. I thank God she
'is off the stage.' What is this but
to say, 'Better the most humdrum
'of existences with the most "re-

spectable of men,' than to be upon
' the stage '?

The volunteered testimony of actors
is both large in bulk and valuable in
quality, and it is all on my side.

Their involuntary testimony I pass
over lightly. Far be from me the
disgusting and ungenerous task of
raking up a heap of the weaknesses,
vanities, and miserablenesses of actors
and actresses dead and gone. After
life's fitful fever they sleep (I trust)
well; and in common candour, it
ought never to be forgotten that
whilst it has always been the fashion
—until one memorable day Mr.
Froude ran amuck of it—for bio-
graphers to shroud their biographees
(the American Minister must bear
the brunt of this word on his broad
shoulders) in a crape veil of respecta-
bility, the records of the stage have
been written in another spirit. We
always know the worst of an actor,

10

seldom his best. David Garrick was a better man than Lord Eldon, and Macready was at least as good as Dickens.

There is however, one portion of this body of involuntary testimony on which I must be allowed to rely, for it may be referred to without offence.

Our dramatic literature is our greatest literature. It is the best thing we have done. Dante may over-top Milton, but Shakespeare surpasses both. He is our finest achievement; his plays our noblest possession; the things in the world most worth thinking about. To live daily in his company, to study his works with minute and loving care —in no spirit of pedantry searching for double endings, but in order to discover their secret, and to make the spoken word tell upon the hearts of man and woman—this might have been expected to produce great intellectual if not moral results.

The most magnificent compliment ever paid by man to woman is undoubtedly Steele's to the Lady Elizabeth Hastings. ' To love her,' wrote he, ' is a liberal education.' As much might surely be said of Shakespeare.

But what are the facts—the ugly, hateful facts? Despite this great advantage—this close familiarity with the noblest and best in our literature—the taste of actors, their critical judgment, always has been and still is, if not beneath contempt, at all events far below the average intelligence of their day. By taste, I do not mean taste in flounces and in furbelows, tunics and stockings; but in the weightier matters of the truly sublime and the essentially ridiculous. Salvini's Macbeth is undoubtedly a fine performance; and yet that great

actor, as the result of his study, has
placed it on record that he thinks
the sleep-walking scene ought to be
assigned to Macbeth instead of to
his wife.   Shades of Shakespeare
and Siddons, what think you of
that?

It is a strange fatality, but a proof
of the inherent pettiness of the actor's
art, that though it places its votary
in the very midst of literary and
artistic influences, and of necessity
'nforms him of the best and worthiest,
he is yet, so far as his own culture is
concerned, left out in the cold—art's
slave, not her child.

What have the devotees of the
drama taught us?   Nothing! it is
we who have taught them.   We go
first, and they come lumbering after.
It was not from the stage the voicc
arose bidding us recognise the su-
premacy of Shakespeare's genius?
Actors first ignored him, then hide·

ously mutilated him ; and though now occasionally compelled, out of deference to the taste of the day, to forego their green-room traditions, to forswear their Tate and Brady emendations, in their heart of hearts they love him not ; and it is with a light step and a smiling face that our great living tragedian flings aside Hamlet's tunic or Shylock's gaberdine to revel in the melodramatic glories of *The Bells* and *The Corsican Brothers.*

Our gratitude is due in this great matter to men of letters, not to actors. If it be asked, ' What have actors to do with literature and criticism?' I answer, ' Nothing;' and add, ' That is my case.'

But the notorious bad taste of actors is not entirely due to their living outside Literature, with its words for ever upon their lips, but none of its truths engraven on their hearts. It may partly be accounted for by the fact that for the purposes of an ambitious actor bad plays are the best.

In reading actors' lives, nothing strikes you more than their delight in making a hit in some part nobody ever thought anything of before. Garrick was proud past all endurance of his Beverley in the *Gamester*, and one can easily see why. Until people saw Garrick's Beverley, they didn't think there was anything in the *Gamester;* nor was there, except what Garrick put there.* This is called creating a part, and he is the greatest actor who creates most parts.

* This illustration is not a very happy one, for as an accomplished critic has pointed out in the *St. James's Gazette*, Moore's play was written especially for Mr. Garrick, and was first made known to the public by Mr. Garrick. The play was, however, subsequently printed, and to be had of all booksellers; and the observations in the text would therefore hold good of anyone who put off seeing the play until he had read it. But whether there was any person so ill-advised I cannot say.

But genius in the author of the play is a terrible obstacle in the way of an actor who aspires to identify himself once and for all with the leading part in it. Mr. Irving may act Hamlet well or ill—and, for my part, I think he acts it exceedingly well—but behind Mr. Irving's Hamlet, as behind everybody else's Hamlet, there looms a greater Hamlet than them all—Shakespeare's Hamlet, the real Hamlet.

But Mr. Irving's Mathias is quite another kettle of fish, all of Mr. Irving's own catching. Who ever, on leaving the Lyceum, after seeing *The Bells,* was heard to exclaim, ' It is all mighty fine ; but that is not my idea of Mathias ' ? Do not we all feel that without Mr. Irving there could be no Mathias ?

We best like doing what we do best : and an actor is not to be blamed for preferring the task of making much of a very little to that of making little of a great deal.

As for actresses, it surely would be the height of ungenerosity to blame a woman for following the only regular profession commanding fame and fortune the kind consideration of man has left open to her. For two centuries women have been free to follow this profession, onerous and exacting though it be, and by doing so have won the rapturous applause of generations of men, who are all ready enough to believe that where their pleasure is involved, no risks of life or honour are too great for a woman to run. It is only when the latter, tired of the shams of life, would pursue the realities, that we become alive to the fact—hitherto, I suppose, studiously concealed from us —how frail and feeble a creature she is.

Lastly, it must not be forgotten that we are discussing a question of casuistry, one which is 'stuff o' the conscience,' and where consequently words are all important.

Is an actor's calling an eminently worthy one?—that is the question. It may be lawful, useful, delightful, but is it worthy?

An actor's life is an artist's life. No artist, however eminent, has more than one life, or does anything worth doing in that life, unless he is prepared to spend it royally in the service of his art, caring for nought else. Is an actor's art worth the price? I answer, No!

A ROGUE'S MEMOIRS.

ONE is often tempted of the devil to forswear the study of history altogether as the pursuit of the Unknowable. 'How is it possible,' he whispers in our ear, as we stand gloomily regarding the portly calf-bound volumes without which no gentleman's library is complete, 'how 'is it possible to suppose that you 'have there, on your shelves— 'the actual facts of history—a true 'record of what men, dead long ago, 'felt and thought ?' Yet, if we have not, I for one, though of a literary turn, would sooner spent my leisure playing skittles with boors than in reading sonorous lies in stout volumes.

'It is not so much,' wilily insinuates the Tempter, 'that these renowned 'authors lack knowledge. Their 'habit of giving an occasional refer- 'ence (though the verification of 'these is usually left to the malig- 'nancy of a rival and less popular 'historian) argues at least some read- 'ing. No; what is wanting is igno- 'rance, carefully acquired and studi- 'ously maintained. This is no para- 'dox. To carry the truisms, theories, 'laws, language of to-day, along with 'you in your historical pursuits, is to 'turn the muse of history upside 'down—a most disrespectful pro- 'ceeding—and yet to ignore them— 'to forget all about them—to 'hang them up with your hat and 'coat in the hall, to remain there 'whilst you sit in the library compos- 'ing your immortal work, which is so

'happily to combine all that is best
'in Gibbon and Macaulay—a sneer-
less Gibbon and an impartial Ma-
'caulay—is a task which, if it be not
'impossible is, at all events, of huge
difficulty.

'Another blemish in English his-
'torical work has been noticed by the
'Rev. Charles Kingsley, and may
'therefore be referred to by me with-
'out offence. Your standard histo-
'rians, having no unnatural regard for
'their most indefatigable readers, the
'wives and daughters of England,
'feel it incumbent upon them to pass
'over, as unfit for dainty ears and
dulcet tones, facts, and rumours of
facts, which none the less often de-
'termined events by stirring the
'strong feelings of your ancestors,
'whose conduct, unless explained by
'this light, must remain enigmatical.

'When, to these anachronisms of
'thought and omissions of fact, you

'have added the dishonesty of the
'partisan historian and the false
'glamour of the picturesque one, you
'will be so good as to proceed to find
'the present value of history!'

Thus far the Enemy of Mankind :

An admirable lady orator is reported lately to have 'brought down'
Exeter Hall by observing, 'in a low
but penetrating voice,' that the devil
was a very stupid person. It is true
that Ben Jonson is on the side of
the lady, but I am far too orthodox
to entertain any such opinion ; and
though I have, in this instance of
history, so far resisted him as to have
refrained from sending my standard
historians to the auction mart—where,
indeed, with the almost single exception of Mr. Grote's History of Greece
(the octavo edition in twelve volumes),
prices rule so low as to make cartage
a consideration—I have still of late
found myself turning off the turnpike

of history to loiter down the primrose
paths of men's memoirs of themselves
and their times.

Here at least, so we argue, we are
comparatively safe. Anachronisms
of thought are impossible ; omissions
out of regard for female posterity un-
likely, and as for party spirit, if found,
it forms part of what lawyers call the
res gestæ, and has therefore a value of
its own. Against the perils of the
picturesque, who will insure us ?

But when we have said all this,
and, sick of prosing, would begin reading, the number of really readable
memoirs is soon found to be but few.
This is, indeed, unfortunate ; for it
launches us off on another prose-
journey by provoking the question,
What makes memoirs interesting ?

Is it necessary that they should be
the record of a noble character ?
Certainly not. We remember Pepys,
who—well, never mind what he does.

We call to mind Cellini ; *he* runs behind a fellow-creature, and with ' admirable address' sticks a dagger in
the nape of his neck, and long afterwards records the fact, almost with
reverence, in his life's story. Can
anything be more revolting than some
portions of the revelation Benjamin
Franklin was pleased to make of
himself in writing ? And what about
Rousseau ? Yet, when we have
pleaded guilty for these men, a
modern Savonarola, who had persuaded us to make a bonfire of their
works, would do well to keep a sharp
look-out, lest at the last moment we
should be found substituting ' Pearson
on the Creed ' for Pepys, Coleridge's
' Friend' for Cellini, John Foster's
Essays for Franklin, and Roget's
Bridgewater Treatise for Rousseau.

Neither will it do to suppose that
the interest of a memoir depends on
its writer having been concerned in

great affairs, or lived in stirring times
The dullest memoirs written even in
English, and not excepting those
maimed records of life known as 'religious biography,' are the work of men
of the ' attaché ' order, who, having
been mixed up in events which the
newspapers of the day chronicled as
' Important Intelligence,' were not
unnaturally led to cherish the belief
that people would like to have from
their pens full, true and particular
accounts of all that then happened,
or, as they, if moderns, would probably prefer to say, transpired.   But
the World, whatever an over-bold
Exeter Hall may say of her old asso-
ciate the Devil, is not a stupid person,
and declines to be taken in twice; and
turning a deaf ear to the most painstaking and trustworthy accounts of de-
ceased Cabinets and silenced Confer-
ences, goes journeying along her broad
way, chuckling over some old joke in

Boswell, and reading with fresh delight the all-about-nothing letters of
Cowper and Lamb.

How then does a man—be he good
or bad—big or little—a philosopher
or a fribble—St. Paul or Horace
Walpole—make his memoirs interesting ?

To say that the one thing needful
is individuality, is not quite enough.
To be an individual is the inevitable,
and in most cases the unenviable, lot
of every child of Adam. Each one
of us has, like a tin soldier, a stand
of his own. To have an individuality
is no sort of distinction, but to be
able to make it felt in writing is not
only distinction but under favouring
circumstances immortality.

Have we not all some correspon-
dents, though probably but few, from
whom we never receive a letter without feeling sure that we shall find inside the envelope something written

that will make us either glow with
the warmth or shiver with the cold
of our correspondent's life? But
how many other people are to be
found, good, honest people too, who
no sooner take pen in hand than they
stamp unreality on every word they
write.   It is a hard fate, but they cannot escape it.   They may be as
literal as the late Earl Stanhope, as
painstaking as Bishop Stubbs, as
much in earnest as Mr. Gladstone
—their lives may be noble, their aims
high, but no sooner do they seek to
narrate to us their story, than we find
it is not to be.   To hearken to them
is past praying for.   We turn from
them as from a guest who has out-
stayed his welcome.   Their writing
wearies, irritates, disgusts.

Here then, at last, we have the
two classes of memoir writers—those
who manage to make themselves felt,
and those who do not.   Of the latter,

a very little is a great deal too much
—of the former we can never have
enough.

What a liar was Benvenuto Cellini!
—who can believe a word he says?
To hang a dog on his oath would be
a judicial murder. Yet when we
lay down his memoirs and let our
thoughts travel back to those far-off
days he tells us of, there we see
him standing, in bold relief, against
the black sky of the past, the very
man he was. Not more surely did
he, with that rare skill of his, stamp
the image of Clement VII. on the
papal currency than he did the im-
press of his own singular personality
upon every word he spoke and every
sentence he wrote.

We ought, of course, to hate him,
but do we? A murderer he has
written himself down. A liar he
stands self-convicted of being. Were
anyone in the nether world bold

enough to call him thief, it may
be doubted whether Rhadamanthus
would award him the damages for
which we may be certain he would
loudly clamour.   Why do we not
hate him ?   Listen to him :

' Upon my uttering these words,
' there was a general outcry, the
' noblemen affirming that I promised
' too much.   But one of them, who
was a great philosopher, said in
' my favour, " From the admirable
' symmetry of shape and happy
' physiognomy of this young man, I
' venture to engage that he will per-
' form all he promises, and more."
' The Pope replied, " I am of the
'same opinion ;" then calling Trajano,
' his gentleman of the bed-chamber,
he ordered him to fetch me five
' hundred ducats.'

And so it always ended ; suspicions,
aroused most reasonably, allayed
most unreasonably, and then—ducats.

He deserved hanging, but he died in
his bed. He wrote his own memoirs
after a fashion that ought to have
brought posthumous justice upon him,
and made them a literary gibbet, on
which he should swing, a creaking
horror, for all time ; but nothing of
the sort has happened. The rascal
is so symmetrical, and his physiognomy, as it gleams upon us
through the centuries, so happy, that
we cannot withhold our ducats,
though we may accompany the gift
with a shower of abuse.

This only proves the profundity of
an observation made by Mr. Bagehot
—a man who carried away into the
next world more originality of thought
than is now to be found in the Three
Estates of the Realm. Whilst re-
marking upon the extraordinary
reputation of the late Francis Horner
and the trifling cost he was put to in
supporting it, Mr. Bagehot said that

it proved the advantage of 'keeping
an atmosphere.'

The common air of heaven
sharpens men's judgments. Poor
Horner, but for that kept atmosphere
of his, always surrounding him, would
have been bluntly asked, 'What he
'had done since he was breeched,'
and in reply he could only have
muttered something about the currency. As for our especial rogue
Cellini, the question would probably
have assumed this shape : 'Rascal,
'name the crime you have not com-
'mitted, and account for the omis-
'sion.'

But these awkward questions are
not put to the lucky people who keep
their own atmospheres. The critics,
before they can get at them, have to
step out of the everyday air, where
only achievements count and the
Decalogue still goes for something,
into the kept atmosphere, which they

have no sooner breathed than they begin to see things differently, and to measure the object thus surrounded with a tape of its own manufacture. Horner—poor, ugly, a man neither of words nor deeds —becomes one of our great men; a nation mourns his loss and erects his statue in the Abbey. Mr. Bagehot gives several instances of the same kind, but he does not mention Cellini, who is, however, in his own way, an admirable example.

You open his book—a Pharisee of the Pharisees. Lying indeed! Why, you hate prevarication. As for murder, your friends know you too well to mention the subject in your hearing, except in immediate connection with capital punishment. You are, of course, willing to make some allowance for Cellini's time and place—the first half of the sixteenth century and Italy. 'Yes, you remark, 'Cellini shall have strict 'justice at my hands.' So you say as you settle yourself in your chair and begin to read. We seem to hear the rascal laughing in his grave. His spirit breathes upon you from his book—peeps at you roguishly as you turn the pages. His atmosphere surrounds you; you smile when you ought to frown, chuckle when you should groan, and—O final triumph —laugh aloud when, if you had a rag of principle left, you would fling the book into the fire. Your poor moral sense turns away with a sigh, and patiently awaits the conclusion of the second volume.

How cautiously does he begin, how gently does he win your ear by his seductive piety! I quote from Mr. Roscoe's translation :—

'It is a duty incumbent on upright 'and credible men of all ranks, who 'have performed anything noble or

' praiseworthy, to record, in their own
' writing, the events of their lives;
' yet they should not commence this
' honourable task before they have
' passed their fortieth year. Such,
' at least, is my opinion, now that I
' have completed my fifty-eighth year,
' and am settled in Florence, where,
' considering the numerous ills that
' constantly attend human life, I per-
' ceive that I have never before been
' so free from vexations and cala-
' mities, or possessed of so great a
' share of content and health as at
' this period. Looking back on some
' delightful and happy events of my
' life, and on many misfortunes so
' truly overwhelming that the appal-
' ling retrospect makes me wonder
' how I have reached this age in
' vigour and prosperity, through
' God's goodness I have resolved to
' publish an account of my life; and
'. . . . I must, in commencing

' my narrative, satisfy the public on
' some few points to which its curio-
' sity is usually directed ; the first of
' which is to ascertain whether a man
' is descended from a virtuous and
' ancient family . . . . I shall
' therefore now proceed to inform
' the reader how it pleased God that
' I should come into the world.'

So you read on page 1 ; what you
read on page 191 is this :—

' Just after sunset, about eight
' o'clock, as this musqueteer stood
' at his door with his sword in his
' hand, when he had done supper, I
' with great address came close up
' to him with a long dagger, and gave
' him a violent back-handed stroke,
' which I aimed at his neck. He
' instantly turned round, and the
' blow, falling directly upon his left
' shoulder, broke the whole bone of
' it ; upon which he dropped his
' sword, quite overcome by the pain,

' and took to his heels. I pursued,
' and in four steps came up with him,
' when, raising the dagger over his
' head, which he lowered down, I hit
' him exactly upon the nape of the
' neck. The weapon penetrated so
' deep that, though I made a great
' effort to recover it again, I found
' it impossible.'

So much for murder. Now for
manslaughter, or rather Cellini's
notion of manslaughter.

' Pompeo entered an apothecary's
' shop at the corner of the Chiavica,
' about some business, and stayed
' there for some time. I was told
' he had boasted of having bullied
' me, but it turned out a fatal ad-
' venture to him. Just as I arrived
' at that quarter he was coming out
' of the shop, and his bravoes, having
' made an opening, formed a circle
' round him. I thereupon clapped
my hand to a sharp dagger, and

' having forced my way through the
' file of ruffians, laid hold of him by
' the throat, so quickly and with such
' presence of mind, that there was
' not one of his friends could defend
' him.   I pulled him towards me to
' give him a blow in front, but he
' turned his face about through excess
' of terror, so that I wounded him
' exactly under the ear ; and upon
' repeating my blow, he fell down
' dead.   It had never been my inten-
' tion to kill him, but blows are not
' always under command.'

We must all feel that it would never
have done to have begun with these
passages, but long before the 191st
page has been reached Cellini has
retreated into his own atmosphere,
and the scales of justice have. been
hopelessly tampered with.

That such a man as this encoun-
tered suffering in the course of his
life, should be matter for satisfaction

to every well-regulated mind; but,
somehow or another, you find yourself pitying the fellow as he narrates
the hardships he endured in the
Castle of S. Angelo. He is so symmetrical a rascal! Just hear him!
listen to what he says well on in the
second volume, after the little inci-
dents already quoted:

'Having at length recovered my
'strength and vigour, after I had
'composed myself and resumed my
'cheerfulness of mind, I continued
'to read my Bible, and so accus-
'tomed my eyes to that darkness,
'that though I was at first able to
'read only an hour and a half, I
'could at length read three hours. I
'then reflected on the wonderful
'power of the Almighty upon the
'hearts of simple men, who had
'carried their enthusiasm so far as to
'believe firmly that God would in-
'dulge them in all they wished for;

'and I promised myself the assist-
'ance of the Most High, as well
'through His mercy as on account
'of my innocence.   Thus turning
'constantly to the Supreme Being,
'sometimes in prayer, sometimes in
''silent meditation on the divine
'goodness, I was totally engrossed
'by these heavenly reflections, and
'came to take such delight in pious
meditations that I no longer thought
of past misfortunes. On the con-
'trary, I was all day long singing
psalms and many other composi-
'tions of mine, in which I celebrated
'and praised the Deity.'

Thus torn from their context, these
passages may seem to supply the
best possible falsification of the previous statement that Cellini told the
truth about himself. Judged by these
passages alone, he may appear a
hypocrite of an unusually odious description. But it is only necessary

to read his book to dispel that notion.
He tells lies about other people; he
repeats long conversations, sounding
his own praises, during which, as his
own narrative shows, he was not
present; he exaggerates his own
exploits, his sufferings—even, it may
be, his crimes; but when we lay
down his book, we feel we are saying good-bye to a man whom we
know.

He has introduced himself to us,
and though doubtless we prefer saints
to sinners, we may be forgiven for
liking the company of a live rogue
better than that of the lay-figures
and empty clock-cases labelled with
distinguished names, who are to be
found doing duty for men in the
works of our standard historians.
What would we not give to know
Julius Cæsar one half as well as we
know this outrageous rascal? The
saints of the earth, too, how shadowy

they are! Which of them do we really know? Excepting one or two ancient and modern Quietists, there is hardly one amongst the whole number who being dead yet speaketh. Their memoirs far too often only reveal to us a hazy something, certainly not recognisable as a man. This is generally the fault of their editors, who, though men themselves, confine their editorial duties to going up and down the diaries and papers of the departed saint, and obliterating all human touches. This they do for the 'better prevention of scandals;' and one cannot deny that they attain their end, though they pay dearly for it.

I shall never forget the start I gave when, on reading some old book about India, I came across an after-dinner jest of Henry Martyn's. The thought of Henry Martyn laughing over the walnuts and the wine was

almost, as Robert Browning's un‧
known painter says, 'too wildly
dear;' and to this day I cannot help
thinking that there must be a mistake
somewhere.

To return to Cellini, and to con-
clude. On laying down his 'Memoirs,'
let us be careful to recall our banished
moral sense, and make peace with
her, by passing a final judgment on
this desperate sinner, which perhaps,
after all, we cannot do better than
by employing language of his own
concerning a monk, a fellow-prisoner
of his, who never, so far as appears,
murdered anybody, but of whom
Cellini none the less felt himself entitled to say :

'I admired his shining qualities,
'but his odious vices I freely cen-
'sured and held in abhorrence.'

12

THE VIA MEDIA.

THE world is governed by logic. Truth as well as Providence is always on the side of the strongest battalions. An illogical opinion only requires rope enough to hang itself.

Middle men may often seem to be earning for themselves a place in Universal Biography, and middle positions frequently seem to afford the final solution of vexed questions; but this double delusion seldom outlives a generation. The world wearies of the men, for, attractive as their characters may be, they are for ever telling us, generally at great length, how it comes about that they stand just where they do, and we soon tire of explanations and forget apologists. The positions, too, once hailed with such acclaim, so eagerly recognized as the true refuges for poor mortals anxious to avoid being run over by fast-driving logicians, how untenable do they soon appear! how quickly do they grow antiquated! how completely they are forgotten!

The Via Media, alluring as is its direction, imposing as are its portals, is, after all, only what Londoners call a blind alley, leading nowhere.

'Ratiocination,' says one of the most eloquent and yet exact of modern writers,* 'is the great principle of 'order in thinking : it reduces a chaos 'into harmony, it catalogues the 'accumulations of krowledge ; it 'maps out for us the relations of 'its separate departments. It en- 'ables the independent intellects of

* Dr. Newman in the 'Grammar of Assent.'

' many acting and re-acting on each
' other to bring their collective force
' to bear upon the same subject-
' matter.   If language is an in-
' estimable gift to man, the logical
' faculty prepares it for our use.
' Though it does not go so far as to
' ascertain truth ; still, it teaches us
' the *direction* in which truth lies, and
' *how propositions lie towards each other.*
' Nor is it a slight benefit to know
' what is needed for the proof of a
' point, what is wanting in a theory,
' how a theory hangs together, *and*
' *what will follow if it be admitted.*'

This great principle of order in
thinking is what we are too apt to
forget.   ' Give us,' cry many, ' safety
' in our opinions, and let who will be
' logical.   An Englishman's creed is
' compromise.   His *bête noire* extrava-
' gance.   We are not saved by syl-
' logism.'   Possibly not ; but yet there
can be no safety in an illogical posi-

tion, and one's chances of snug quarters in eternity cannot surely be bettered by our believing at one and the same moment of time self-con-tradictory propositions.

But, talk as we may, for the bulk of mankind it will doubtless always remain true that a truth does not ex-clude its contradictory. Darwin and Moses are both right. Between the Gospel according to Matthew and the Gospel according to Matthew Arnold there is no difference.

If the too apparent absurdity of this is pressed home, the baffled illogician, persecuted in one position, flees into another, and may be heard assuring his tormentor that in a period like the present, which is so notoriously transitional, a logician is as much out of place as a bull in a china shop, and that unless he is quiet, and keeps his tail well wrapped round his legs, the mischief he will do to his neigh-

bours' china creeds and delicate porce
lain opinions is shocking to contem-
plate. But this excuse is no longer ad-
missible. The age has remained transitional so unconscionably long, that
we cannot consent to forego the use
of logic any longer. For a decade or
two it was all well enough, but when
it comes to four-score years, one's
patience gets exhausted. Carlyle's
celebrated Essay, ' Characteristics,'
in which this transitional period is
diagnosed with unrivalled acumen, is
half a century old. Men have been
born in it—have grown old in it—
have died in it. It has outlived the
old Court of Chancery. It is high
time the spurs of logic were applied
to its broken-winded sides.

Notwithstanding the obstinate preference the ' bulk of mankind ' always
show for demonstrable errors over
undeniable truths, the number of
persons is daily increasing who have

begun to put a value upon mental coherency and to appreciate the charm of a logical position.

It was common talk at one time to express astonishment at the extending influence of the Church of Rome, and to wonder how people who went about unaccompanied by keepers could submit their reason to the Papacy, with her open rupture with science and her evil historical reputation. From astonishment to contempt is but a step. We first open wide our eyes and then our mouths.

' Lord So-and-so, his coat bedropt with wax,
All Peter's chains about his waist, his back
Brave with the needlework of Noodledom,
Believes, —who wonders and who cares?'

It used to be thought a sufficient explanation to say either that the man was an ass or that it was all those Ritualists. But gradually it became apparent that the pervert was not always an ass, and that the

Ritualists had nothing whatever to do with it. If a man's tastes run in the direction of Gothic Architecture, free seats, daily services, frequent communions, lighted candles and Church millinery, they can all be gratified, not to say glutted, in the Church of his baptism.

It is not the Roman ritual, however splendid, nor her ceremonial, however spiritually significant, nor her system of doctrine, as well arranged as Roman law and as subtle as Greek philosophy, that makes Romanists nowadays.

It is when a person of religious spirit and strong convictions as to the truth and importance of certain dogmas—few in number it may be; perhaps only one, the Being of God —first becomes fully alive to the tendency and direction of the most active opinions of the day; when, his alarm quickening his insight, he reads

as it were between the lines of books,
magazines, and newspapers; when,
struck with a sudden trepidation, he
asks, 'Where is this to stop? how
'can I, to the extent of a poor
'ability, help to stem this tide of
'opinion which daily increases its
'volume and floods new territory?'—
then it is that the Church of Rome
stretches out her arms and seems to
say, 'Quarrel not with your destiny,
'which is to become a Catholic.
'You may see difficulties and you
'may have doubts. They abound
'everywhere. You will never get rid
'of them. But I, and I alone, have
'never coquetted with the spirit of the
'age. I, and I alone, have never
'submitted my creeds to be over-
'hauled by infidels. Join me, ac-
'knowledge my authority, and you
'need dread no side attack and fear
'no charge of inconsistency. Succeed
finally I must, but even were I to

fail, yours would be the satisfaction
' of knowing that you had never held
' an opinion, used an argument, or
' said a word, that could fairly have
' served the purpose of your trium-
' phant enemy.'

At such a crisis as this in a man's
life, he does not ask himself, How
little can I believe? With how few
miracles can I get off?—he demands
sound armour, sharp weapons, and,
above all, firm ground to stand on—
a good footing for his faith—and
these he is apt to fancy he can get
from Rome alone.

No doubt he has to pay for them,
but the charm of the Church of
Rome is this: when you have paid
her price you get your goods—a neat
assortment of coherent, inter-depen-
dent, logical opinions.

It is not much use, under such
circumstances, to call the convert a
coward, and facetiously to inquire of

him what he really thinks about St.
Januarius. Nobody ever began with
Januarius. I have no doubt a good
many Romanists would be glad to
be quit of him. He is part of the
price they have to pay in order that
their title to the possession of other
miracles may be quieted. If you can
convince the convert that he can dis-
believe Januarius of Naples without
losing his grip of Paul of Tarsus, you
will be well employed ; but if you
begin with merry gibes, and end
with contemptuously demanding that
he should have done with such nonsense and fling the rubbish overboard,
he will draw in his horns and perhaps,
if he knows his Browning, murmur
to himself :—

'To such a process, I discern no end.
 Cutting off one excrescence to see two ;
 There is ever a next in size, now grown as big,
 That meets the knife. I cut and cut again ;
 First cut the Liquefaction, what comes last
 But Fichte's clever cut at God Himself ?'

To suppose that no person is logically entitled to fear God and to ridicule Januarius at the same time, is doubtless extravagant, but to do so requires care. There is an 'order ' in thinking. We must consider ' how propositions lie towards each ' other—how a theory hangs together, ' and what will follow if it be ad- ' mitted.'

It is eminently desirable that we should consider the logical termini of our opinions. Travelling up to town last month from the West, a gentleman got into my carriage at Swindon who, as we moved off and began to rush through the country, became unable to restrain his delight at our speed. His face shone with pride, as if he were pulling us himself. ' What ' a charming train !' he exclaimed. ' This is the pace I like to travel at.' I indicated assent. Shortly afterwards, when our windows rattled as

we rushed through Reading, he let
one of them down in a hurry, and
cried out in consternation, ' Why, I
' want to get out here.' 'Charming
' train,' I observed. 'Just the pace
' I like to travel at ; but it *is* awkward
' if you want to go anywhere except
' Paddington.' My companion made
no reply; his face ceased to shine, and
as he sat whizzing past his dinner,
I mentally compared his recent exul-
tation with that of those who in
the present day extol much of its
spirit, use many of its arguments, and
partake in most of its triumphs, in
utter ignorance as to whitherwards
it is all tending as surely as the Great
Western rails run into Paddington.
' Poor victims !' said a distinguished
Divine, addressing the Evangelicals,
then rejoicing over their one legal
victory, the ' Gorham Case'; ' do
' you dream that the spirit of the age
' is working for you, or are you

secretly prepared to go further than
'you avow ?'

Mr. Matthew Arnold's friends, the
Nonconformists, are, as a rule, nowadays, bad logicians.   What Dr.
Newman has said of the Tractarians
is (with but a verbal alteration) also
true of a great many Nonconformists :
' Moreover, there are those among
' them who have very little grasp of
' principle, even from the natural
' temper of their minds.   They see
' this thing is beautiful, and that is
' in the Fathers, and a third is ex-
' pedient, and a fourth pious ; but of
' their connection one with another,
' their hidden essence and their life,
' and the bearing of external matters
' upon each and upon all, they have
' no perception or even suspicion.
' They do not look at things as part
' of a whole, and often will sacrifice
' the most important and precious
' portions of their creed, or make

' irremediable concessions in word
' or in deed, from mere simplicity and
' want of apprehension.'

We have heard of grown-up
Baptists asked to become, and
actually becoming, godfathers and
godmothers to Episcopalian babies !
What terrible confusion is here ! A
point is thought to be of sufficient
importance to justify separation on
account of it from the whole Christian
Church, and yet not to be of importance enough to debar the separatist
from taking part in a ceremony whose
sole significance is that it gives the
lie direct to the point of separation.

But we all of us—Churchmen and
Dissenters alike—select our opinions
far too much in the same fashion as
ladies are reported, I dare say quite
falsely, to do their afternoon's shop-
ping—this thing because it is so
pretty, and that thing because it is
so cheap. We pick and choose, take

and leave, approbate and reprobate
in a breath. A familiar anecdote is
never out of place : An English
captain, anxious to conciliate a savage
king, sent him on shore, for his own
royal wear, an entire dress suit. His
majesty was graciously pleased to
accept the gift, and as it never occurred to the royal mind that he
could, by any possibility, wear all the
things himself, with kingly generosity
he distributed what he did not want
amongst his Court. This done, he
sent for the donor to thank him in
person. As the captain walked up
the beach, his majesty advanced to
meet him, looking every inch a king
in the sober dignity of a dress-coat.
The waistcoat imparted an air of
pensive melancholy that mightily
became the Prime Minister, whilst
the Lord Chamberlain, as he skipped
to and fro in his white gloves, looked
a courtier indeed. The trousers had

become the subject of an unfortunate dispute, in the course of which they had sustained such injuries as to be hardly recognisable. The captain was convulsed with laughter.

But, in truth, the mental toilet of most of us is as defective and almost as risible as was that of this savage Court. We take on our opinions without paying heed to conclusions, and the result is absurd. Better be without any opinions at all. A naked savage is not necessarily an un-dignified object; but a savage in a dress-coat and nothing else is, and must ever remain, a mockery and a show. There is a great relativity about a dress-suit. In the language of the logicians, the name of each article not only denotes that par-ticular, but connotes all the rest. Hence it came about that that which, when worn in its entirety, is so dull and decorous, became so provocative

13

of Homeric laughter when distributed amongst several wearers.

No person with the least tincture of taste can ever weary of Dr. Newman, and no apology is therefore offered for another quotation from his pages. In his story, ' Loss and Gain,' he makes one of his characters, who has just become a Catholic, thus refer to the stock Anglican Divines, a class of writers who are, at all events, immensely superior to the Ellicotts and Farrars of these latter days : ' I am embracing that creed ' which upholds the divinity of tradi- ' tion with Laud, consent of Fathers ' with Beveridge, a visible Church ' with Bramhall, dogma with Bull, ' the authority of the Pope with ' Thorndyke, penance with Taylor, ' prayers for the dead with Ussher, ' celibacy, asceticism, ecclesiastical ' discipline with Bingham.' What is this to say but that, according to the

Cardinal, our great English divines have divided the Roman dress-suit amongst themselves?

This particular charge may perhaps be untrue, but with that I am not concerned. If it is not true of them, it is true of somebody else 'That is satisfactory so far as Mr. Lydgate is concerned,' says Mrs. Farebrother in 'Middlemarch,' with an air of precision ; 'but as to Bulstrode, the report may be true of some other son.'

We must all be acquainted with the reckless way in which people pluck opinions like flowers—a bud here, and a leaf there. The bouquet is pretty to-day, but you must look for it to-morrow in the oven.

There is a sense in which it is quite true, what our other Cardinal has said about Ultramontanes, Anglicans, and Orthodox Dissenters all being in the same boat. They all of

them enthrone Opinion, holding it to
be, when encased in certain dogmas,
Truth Absolute. Consequently they
have all their martyrologies — the
bright roll-call of those who have
defied Cæsar even unto death, or at
all events gaol. They all, therefore,
put something above the State, and
apply tests other than those recognised in our law courts.

The precise way by which they
come at their opinions is only detail.
Be it an infallible Church, an infallible Book, or an inward spiritual
grace, the outcome is the same. The
Romanist, of course, has to bear the
first brunt, and is the most obnoxious
to the State ; but he must be slow of
comprehension and void of imagination who cannot conceive of circumstances arising in this country when
the State should assert it to be its
duty to violate what even Protestants
believe to be the moral law of God.

Therefore, in opposing Ultramon-
tanism, as it surely ought to be op-
posed, care ought to be taken by
those who are not prepared to go all
lengths with Cæsar, to select their
weapons of attack, not from his
armoury, but from their own.

How ridiculous it is to see some
estimable man who subscribes to the
Bible Society, and takes what he
calls 'a warm interest' in the heathen,
chuckling over some scoffing article
in a newspaper—say about a Church
Congress—and never perceiving, so
unaccustomed is he to examine directions, that he is all the time laughing
at his own folly! Aunt Nesbit, in
' Dred,' considered Gibbon a very
pious writer. 'I am sure,' says she,
' he makes the most religious reflec-
' tions all along. I liked him particu
larly on that account.' This poor
lady had some excuse. A vein of irony
like Gibbon's is not struck upon every

day; but readers of newspapers, when they laugh, ought to be able to perceive what it is they are laughing at.

Logic is the prime necessity of the hour. Decomposition and transformation is going on all around us, but far too slowly. Some opinions, bold and erect as they may still stand, are in reality but empty shells. One shove would be fatal. Why is it not given?

The world is full of doleful creatures, who move about demanding our sympathy. I have nothing to offer them but doses of logic, and stern commands to move on or fall back. Catholics in distress about Infallibility; Protestants devoting themselves to the dismal task of paring down the dimensions of this miracle, and reducing the credibility of that one—as if any appreciable relief from the burden of faith could be so obtaiued ; sentimental sceptics, who, after labouring to demolish what they call the chimera of superstition, fall to weeping as they remember they have now no lies to teach their children ; democrats who are frightened at the rough voice of the people and aristocrats flirting with democracy. Logic, if it cannot cure, might at least silence these gentry.

FALSTAFF.*

THERE is more material for a life ol Falstaff than for a life of Shakespeare, though for both there is a lamentable dearth. The difficulties of the biographer are, however, different in the two cases. There is nothing, or next to nothing, in Shakespeare's works which throws light on his own story; and such evidence as we have is of the kind called circumstantial. But Falstaff constantly gives us reminiscences or allusions to his earlier life, and his companions also tell us stories which ought to help us in a biography. The evidence, such as it is, is direct; and the only inference

* This Essay is by 'another hand.'

we have to draw is that from the statement to the truth of the statement.

It has been justly remarked by Sir
James Stephen, that this very inference is perhaps the most difficult
one of all to draw correctly. The
inference from so-called circumstantial evidence, if you have enough
of it, is much surer; for whilst facts
cannot lie, witnesses can, and frequently do. The witnesses on whom
we have to rely for the facts are
Falstaff and his companions—especially Falstaff.

When an old man tries to tell you
the story of his youth, he sees the
facts through a distorting subjective
medium, and gives an impression of
his history and exploits more or less
at variance with the bare facts as
seen by a contemporary outsider.
The scientific Goethe, though truthful enough in the main, certainly fails
in his reminiscences to tell a plain
unvarnished tale. And Falstaff was

not habitually truthful. Indeed, that Western American, who wrote affec-tionately on the tomb of a comrade, 'As a truth-crusher he was un-rivalled,' had probably not given suf-ficient attention to Falstaff's claims in this matter. Then Falstaff's com-panions are not witnesses above sus-picion. Generally speaking, they lie open to the charge made by P. P. against the wags of his parish, that they were men delighting more in their own conceits than in the truth. These are some of our difficulties, and we ask the reader's indulgence in our endeavours to overcome them. We will tell the story from our hero's birth, and will not begin longer *before* that event than is usual with bio-graphers.

The question, *Where* was Falstaff born? has given us some trouble. We confess to having once entertained a strong opinion that he was a Devonshire man. This opinion was based simply on the flow and fertility of his wit. as shown in his conversation, and the rapid and fantastic play of his imagination. But we sought in vain for any verbal provincialisms in support of this theory, and there was something in the character of the man that rather went against it. Still, we clung to the opinion, till we found that philology was against us, and that the Falstaffs unquestionably came from Norfolk.

The name is of Scandinavian origin; and we find in 'Domesday' that a certain Falstaff held freely from the king a church at Stamford. These facts are of great importance. The thirst for which Falstaff was always conspicuous was no doubt inherited —was, in fact, a Scandinavian thirst. The pirates of early English times drank as well as they fought, and their descendants who invade Eng-

land—now that the war of commerce
has superseded the war of conquest—
still bring the old thirst with them,
as anyone can testify who has enjoyed the hospitality of the London
Scandinavian Club. Then this church
was no doubt a familiar landmark in
the family; and when Falstaff stated,
late in life, that if he hadn't forgotten
what the inside of a church was like,
he was a peppercorn and a brewer's
horse, he was thinking with some
remorse of the family temple.

Of the family between the Conquest and Falstaff's birth we know
nothing, except that, according to
Falstaff's statement, he had a grand-
father who left him a seal-ring worth
forty marks. From this statement
we might infer that the ring was an
heirloom, and consequently that Falstaff was an eldest son, and the head
of his family. But we must be careful in drawing our inferences, foi

Prince Henry frequently told Falstaff that the ring was copper; and on one occasion, when Falstaff alleged that his pocket had been picked at the Boar's Head, and this seal-ring and three or four bonds of forty pounds apiece abstracted, the Prince assessed the total loss at eightpence.

After giving careful attention to the evidence, and particularly to the conduct of Falstaff on the occasion of the alleged robbery, we come to the conclusion that the ring *was* copper, and was not an heirloom. This leaves us without any information about Falstaff's family prior to his birth. He was born (as he himself informs the Lord Chief Justice) about three o'clock in the afternoon, with a white head and something a round belly. Falstaff's corpulence, therefore, as well as his thirst, was congenital. Let those who are not born with his comfortable figure sigh in vain to attain his stately proportions. This is a thing which Nature gives us at our birth as much as the Scandinavian thirst or the shaping spirit of imagination.

Born somewhere in Norfolk, Falstaff's early months and years were no doubt rich with the promise of his after greatness. We have no record of his infancy, and are tempted to supply the gap with Rabelais' chapters on Gargantua's babyhood. But regard for the truth compels us to add nothing that cannot fairly be deduced from the evidence. We leave the strapping boy in his swaddling-clothes to answer the question *when* he was born. Now, it is to be regretted that Falstaff, who was so precise about the hour of his birth, should not have mentioned the year. On this point we are again left to inference from con-

flicting statements. We have this
distinct point to start from, that Falstaff, in or about the year 1401, gives
his age as some fifty or by'r Lady in-
clining to three-score. It is true
that in other places he represents
himself as old, and again in another
states that he and his accomplices in
the Gadshill robbery are in the
vaward of their youth. The Chief
Justice reproves him for this affecta-
tion of youth, and puts a question
(which, it is true, elicits no admission
from Falstaff) as to whether every
part of him is not blasted with an-
tiquity.

We are inclined to think that Falstaff rather understated his age when
he described himself as by'r Lady in-
clining to three-score, and that we
shall not be far wrong if we set down
1340 as the year of his birth. We
cannot be certain to a year or two.
There is a similar uncertainty about

the year of Sir Richard Whittington's birth. But both these great men, whose careers afford in some respects striking contrasts, were born within a few years of the middle of the fourteenth century.

Falstaff's childhood was no doubt spent in Norfolk; and we learn from his own lips that he plucked geese, played truant, and whipped top, and that he did not escape beating. That he had brothers and sisters we know; for he tells us that he is *John* with them and *Sir John* with all Europe. We do not know the dame or pedant who taught his young idea how to shoot and formed his manners; but Falstaff says that *if* his manners became him not, he was a fool that taught them him. This does not throw much light on his early education: for it is not clear that the remark applies to that period, and in any case it is purely hypothetical.

But Falstaff, like so many boys since his time, left his home in the country and came to London. His brothers and sisters he left behind him, and we hear no more of them. Probably none of them ever attained eminence, as there is no record of Falstaff's having attempted to borrow money of them. We know Falstaff so well as a tun of man, a horse-back-breaker, and so forth, that it is not easy to form an idea of what he was in his youth. But if we trace back the sack-stained current of his life to the day when, full of wonder and hope, he first rode into London, we shall find him as different from Shakespeare's picture of him as the Thames at Iffley is from the Thames at London Bridge. His figure was shapely; he had no difficulty *then* in seeing his own knee, and if he was not able, as he afterwards asserted, to creep through an alderman's ring, neverthe-

14

less he had all the grace and activity
of youth.   He was just such a lad (tc
take a description almost contempo·
rary) as the Squier who rode with the
Canterbury Pilgrims:

'A lover and a lusty bacheler,
With lockes crull as they were laid in presse,
Of twenty yere of age he was, I gesse.
Of his stature he was of even lengthe,
And wonderly deliver, and grete of strengthe.
    *   *   *   *   *   *
    Embrouded was he, as it were a mede,
All ful of freshe floures, white and rede;
Singing he was, or floyting alle the day,
He was as freshe as is the moneth of May.
Short was his goune, with sleves long and wide,
Wel coude he sitte on hors, and fayre ride,
He coude songes make, and wel endite,
Juste and eke dance, and wel pourtraie and write.
So hot he loved that by nightertale,
He slep no more than doth the nightingale.'

Such was Falstaff at the age of
twenty, or something earlier, when he
entered at Clement's Inn, where were
many other young men reading law,
and preparing for their call to the
Bar.   How much law he read it is
impossible now to ascertain.   That

he had, in later life, a considerable knowledge of the subject is clear, but this may have been acquired like Mr. Micawber's, by experience, as defendant on civil process. We are inclined to think he read but little. *Amici fures temporis:* and he had many friends at Clement's Inn who were not smugs, nor, indeed, reading men in any sense. There was John Doit of Staffordshire, and Black George Barnes, and Francis Pickbone, and Will Squele, a Cotswold man, and Robert Shallow from Gloucestershire. Four of these were such swinge-bucklers as were not to be found again in all the Inns o' Court, and we have it on the authority of Justice Shallow that Falstaff was a good backswordsman, and that before he had done growing he broke the head of Skogan at the Court gate. This Skogan appears to have been Court-jester to Edward III. No doubt the natural rivalry between the amateur and the professional caused the quarrel, and Skogan must have been a good man if he escaped with a broken head only, and without damage to his reputation as a professional wit. The same day that Falstaff did this deed of daring—the only one of the kind recorded of him—Shallow fought with Sampson Stockfish, a fruiterer, behind Gray's Inn. Shallow was a gay dog in his youth, according to his own account: he was called Mad Shallow, Lusty Shallow—indeed, he was called anything. He played Sir Dagonet in Arthur's show at Mile End Green; and no doubt Falstaff and the rest of the set were cast for other parts in the same pageant. These tall fellows of Clement's Inn kept well together, for they liked each other's company, and they needed each other's help in a row in Turnbull Street or elsewhere.

Their watchword was 'Hem, boys!'
and they made the old Strand ring
with their songs as they strolled home
to their chambers of an evening.
They heard the chimes at midnight
—which, it must be confessed, does
not seem to us a desperately dissi-
pated entertainment. But midnight
was a late hour in those days. The
paralytic masher of the present day,
who is most alive at midnight, rises
at noon. *Then* the day began earlier
with a long morning, followed by a
pleasant period called the forenoon.
Under modern conditions we spend
the morning in bed, and to palliate
our sloth call the forenoon and most
of the rest of the day, the morning.
These young men of Clement's Inn
were a lively, not to say a rowdy, set.
They would do anything that led to
mirth or mischief. What passed
when they lay all night in the wind-
mill in St. George's Field we do not

quite know; but we are safe in assuming that they did not go there to pursue their legal duties, or to grind corn. Anyhow, forty years after, that night raised pleasant memories.

John Falstaff was the life and centre of this set, as Robert Shallow was the butt of it. The latter had few personal attractions. According to Falstaff's portrait of him, he looked like a man made after supper of a cheese-paring. When he was naked he was for all the world like a forked radish, with a head fantastically carved upon it with a knife : he was so forlorn that his dimensions to any thick sight were invincible: he was the very genius of famine ; and a certain section of his friends called him mandrake : he came ever in the rearward of the fashion, and sung those tunes to the over-scutched huswives that he heard the carmen whistle, and sware they were his fancies or his good-nights. Then he had the honour of having his head burst by John o' Gaunt, for crowding among the Marshal's men in the Tilt-yard, and this was matter for continual gibe from Falstaff and the other boys. Falstaff was in the van of the fashion, was witty him-self without being at that time the cause that wit was in others. No one could come within range of his wit without being attracted and over-powered. Late in life Falstaff de-plores nothing so much in the character of Prince John of Lancaster as this, that a man cannot make him laugh. He felt this defect in the Prince's character keenly, for laughter was Falstaff's familiar spirit, which never failed to come at his call. It was by laughter that young Falstaff fascinated his friends and ruled over them. There are only left to us a few scraps of his conversation, and these have been, and will be, to all time the delight of all good men. The Clement's Inn boys who enjoyed the feast, of which we have but the crumbs left to us, were happy almost beyond the lot of man. For there is more in laughter than is allowed by the austere, or generally recognised by the jovial. By laughter man is distinguished from the beasts, but the cares and sorrows of life have all but deprived man of this distinguish-ing grace, and degraded him to a brutal solemnity. Then comes (alas, how rarely!) a genius such as Fal-staff's, which restores the power of laughter and transforms the stolid brute into man. This genius ap-proaches nearly to the divine power of creation, and we may truly say, 'Some for less were deified.' It is no marvel that young Falstaff's friends assidu-ously served the deity who gave them this good gift. At first he was satisfied with the mere exercise of his genial power, but he afterwards made it serviceable to him. It was but just that he should receive tribute from those who were beholden to him, for a pleasure which no other could confer.

It was now that Falstaff began to recognise what a precious gift was his congenital Scandinavian thirst, and to lose no opportunity of gratifying it. We have his mature views on education, and we may take them as an example of the general truth that old men habitually advise a young one to shape the conduct of his life after their own. Rightly to apprehend the virtues of sherris-sack is the first qualification in an instructor of youth. 'If I had a 'thousand sons,' says he, 'the first 'humane principles I would teach 'them should be to forswear thin 'potations, and to addict themselves

'to sack'; and further: 'There's
'never none of these demure boys
'come to any proof; for their drink
'doth so over-cool their blood, and
'making many fish-meals, that they
'fall into a kind of male green sick-
'ness; and then when they marry
'they get wenches: they are generally
'fools and cowards, which some of
'us should be too but for inflamma-
'tion.' There can be no doubt that
Falstaff did not in early life over-cool
his blood, but addicted himself to
sack, and gave the subject a great
part of his attention for all the re-
mainder of his days.

It may be that he found the subject too absorbing to allow of his
giving much attention to old Father
Antic the Law. At any rate, he was
never called to the Bar, and posterity
cannot be too thankful that his great
mind was not lost in 'the abyss of
'legal eminence' which has received

so many men who might have adorned their country. That he was fitted for a brilliant legal career can admit of no doubt. His power of detecting analogies in cases apparently different, his triumphant handling of cases apparently hopeless, his wonderful readiness in reply, and his dramatic instinct, would have made him a powerful advocate. It may have been owing to difficulties with the Benchers of the period over questions of discipline, or it may have been a distaste for the profession itself, which induced him to throw up the law and adopt the profession of arms.

We know that while he was still at Clement's Inn he was page to Lord Thomas Mowbray, who was afterwards created Earl of Nottingham and Duke of Norfolk. It must be admitted that here (as elsewhere in Shakespeare) there is some little chronological difficulty. We will not inquire too curiously, but simply accept the testimony of Justice Shallow on the point. Mowbray was an able and ambitious lord, and Falstaff, as page to him, began his military career with every advantage. The French wars of the later years of Edward III. gave frequent and abundant opportunity for distinction. Mowbray distinguished himself in Court and in camp, and we should like to believe that Falstaff was in the sea-fight when Mowbray defeated the French fleet and captured vast quantities of sack from the enemy. Unfortunately, there is no record whatever of Falstaff's early military career, and beyond his own ejaculation, ' Would to God that my name ' was not so terrible to the enemy as ' it is !' and the (possible) inference from it that he must have made his name terrible in some way, we have no evidence that he was ever in the

field before the battle of Shrewsbury.
Indeed, the absence of evidence on
this matter goes strongly to prove the
negative. Falstaff boasts of his
valour, his alacrity, and other qualities
which were not apparent to the casual
observer, but he never boasts of his
services in battle. If there had been
anything of the kind to which he
could refer with complacency, there
is no moral doubt that he would have
mentioned it freely, adding such em-
bellishments and circumstances as
he well knew how.

In the absence of evidence as to
the course of his life, we are left to
conjecture how he spent the forty
years, more or less, between the time
of his studies at Clement's Inn and
the day when Shakespeare introduces
him to us. We have no doubt that
he spent all, or nearly all, this time
in London. His habits were such
as are formed by life in a great city:

his conversation betrays a man who
has lived, as it were, in a crowd, and
the busy haunts of men were the appropriate scene for the display of his
great qualities.   London, even then,
was a great city, and the study of it
might well absorb a lifetime.   Falstaff
knew it well, from the Court, with
which he always preserved a connection, to the numerous taverns where
he met his friends and eluded his
creditors.   The Boar's Head in East-
cheap was his headquarters, and,
like Barnabee's, two centuries later,
his journeys were from tavern to
tavern ; and, like Barnabee, he might
say ' *Multum bibi, nunquam pransi.*'
To begin with, no doubt the dinner
bore a fair proportion to the fluid
which accompanied it, but by degrees
the liquor encroached on and superseded the viands, until his tavern
bills took the shape of the one pur-
loined by Prince Henry, in which

there was but one halfpenny-worth
of bread to an intolerable deal of
sack. It was this inordinate con-
sumption of sack (and not sighing
and grief, as he suggests) which blew
him up like a bladder. A life of
leisure in London always had, and
still has, its temptations. Falstaff's
means were described by the Chief
Justice of Henry IV. as very slender,
but this was after they had been
wasted for years. Originally they
were more ample, and gave him the
opportunity of living at ease with his
friends. No domestic cares disturbed
the even tenor of his life. Bardolph
says he was better accommodated
than with a wife. Like many another
man about town, he thought about
settling down when he was getting
up in years. He weekly swore, so he
tells us, to marry old Mistress Ursula,
but this was only after he saw the
first white hair on his chin. But he

never led Mistress Ursula to the altar.
The only other women for whom he
formed an early attachment were
Mistress Quickly, the hostess of the
Boar's Head, and Doll Tearsheet,
who is described by the page as a
proper gentlewoman, and a kins-
woman of his master's. There is
no denying that Falstaff was on terms
of intimacy with Mistress Quickly,
but he never admitted that he made
her an offer of marriage. She, however, asserted it in the strongest
terms, and with a wealth of circum-
stance.

We must transcribe her story:
'Thou didst swear to me upon a
'parcel-gilt goblet, sitting in my
'Dolphin-chamber, at the round
'table, by a sea-coal fire, upon Wed-
'nesday in Whitsun-week, when the
'Prince broke thy head for liking his
'father to a singing-man of Windsor;
'thou didst swear to me then, as I

'was washing thy wound, to marry
'me, and make me my lady thy
'wife. Canst thou deny it? Did
'not goodwife Keech, the butcher's
'vife, come in then, and call me
'Gossip Quickly? coming in to
'borrow a mess of vinegar; telling us
'she had a good dish of prawns;
'whereby thou didst desire to eat
'some; whereby I told thee they
'were ill for a green wound? And
'didst thou not, when she was gone
'downstairs, desire me to be no more
'familiarity with such poor people;
'saying ere long they should call
'me madam? And didst thou not
'kiss me, and bid me fetch thee
'thirty shillings? I put thee now
'to thy book-oath; deny it if thou
'canst!'

We feel no doubt that if Mistress
Quickly had given this evidence in
action for breach of promise of
marriage, and goodwife Keech corro-

15

borated it, the jury would have found a verdict for the plaintiff, unless indeed they brought in a special verdict to the effect that Falstaff made the promise, but never intended to keep it. But Mistress Quickly contented herself with upbraiding Falstaff, and he cajoled her with his usual skill, and borrowed more money of her.

Falstaff's attachment for Doll Tearsheet lasted many years, but did not lead to matrimony. From the Clement's Inn days till he was threescore he lived in London celibate, and his habits and amusements were much like those of other single gentlemen about town of his time, or, for that matter, of ours. He had only himself to care for, and he cared for himself well. Like his page, he had a good angel about him, but the devil outbid him. He was as virtuously given as other folk, but perhaps the devil had a handle for tempta-

tion in that congenital thirst of his.
He was a social spirit too, and he
tells us that company, villainous company, was the spoil of him. He was
less than thirty when he took the
faithful Bardolph into his service,
and only just past that age when he
made the acquaintance of the nimble
Poins. Before he was forty he became the constant guest of Mistress
Quickly. Pistol and Nym were later
acquisitions, and the Prince did not
come upon the scene till Falstaff was
an old man and knighted.

There is some doubt as to when he
obtained this honour. Richard II.
bestowed titles in so lavish a manner
as to cause discontent among many
who didn't receive them. In 1377,
immediately on his accession, the
earldom of Nottingham was given to
Thomas Mowbray, and on the same
day three other earls and nine knights
were created. We have not been

able to discover the names of these knights, but we confidently expect to unearth them some day, and to find the name of Sir John Falstaff among them. We have already stated that Falstaff had done no service in the field at this time, so he could not have earned his title in that manner. No doubt he got it through the influence of Mowbray, who was in a position to get good things for his friends as well as for himself. It was but a poor acknowledgment for the inestimable benefit of occasionally talking with Falstaff over a quart of sack.

We will not pursue Falstaff's life further than this. It can from this point be easily collected. It is a thankless task to paraphrase a great and familiar text. To attempt to tell the story in better words than Shakespeare would occur to no one but Miss Braddon, who has epitomised Sir Walter, or to Canon Farrar, who has elongated the Gospels. But we feel bound to add a few words as to character. There are, we fear, a number of people who regard Falstaff as a worthless fellow, and who would refrain (if they could) from laughing at his jests. These people do not understand his claim to grateful and affectionate regard. He did more to produce that mental condition of which laughter is the expression than any man who ever lived. But for the cheering presence of him, and men like him, this vale of tears would be a more terrible dwelling-place than it is. In short, Falstaff has done an immense deal to alleviate misery and promote positive happiness. What more can be said of your heroes and philanthropists?

It is, perhaps, characteristic of this commercial age that benevolence should be always associated, if not considered synonymous, with the giving of money. But this is clearly mistaken, for we have to consider what effect the money given produces on the minds and bodies of human beings. Sir Richard Whittington was an eminently benevolent man, and spent his money freely for the good of his fellow-citizens. (We sincerely hope, by the way, that he lent some of it to Falstaff without security.) He endowed hospitals and other charities. Hundreds were relieved by his gifts, and thousands (perhaps) are now in receipt of his alms. This is well. Let the sick and the poor, who enjoy his hospitality and receive his doles, bless his memory. But how much wider and further-reaching is the influence of Falstaff! Those who enjoy his good things are not only the poor and the sick, but all who speak the English language. Nay, more; translation has made him the inheritance of the world, and the benefactor of the entire human race.

It may be, however, that some other nations fail fully to understand and appreciate the mirth and the character of the man. A Dr. G. G. Gervinus, of Heidelberg, has written, in the German language, a heavy work on Shakespeare, in which he attacks Falstaff in a very solemn and determined manner, and particularly charges him with selfishness and want of conscience. We are inclined to set down this malignant attack to envy. Falstaff is the author and cause of universal laughter. Dr. Gervinus will never be the cause of anything universal; but, so far as his influence extends, he produces headaches. It is probably a painful sense of this contrast that goads on the author of headaches to attack the author of laughter.

But is there anything in the charge? We do not claim anything like perfection, or even saintliness, for Falstaff. But we may say of him, as Byron says of Venice, that his very vices are of the gentler sort. And as for this charge of selfishness and want of conscience, we think that the words of Bardolph on his master's death are an overwhelming answer to it. Bardolph said, on hearing the news: 'I would I were with him wheresoever he is: whether he be in heaven or hell.' Bardolph was a mere serving-man, not of the highest sensibility, and he for thirty years knew his master as his valet knows the hero. Surely the man who could draw such an expression of feeling from his rough servant is not the man to be lightly charged with selfishness! Which of us can hope for such an epitaph, not from a hireling, but from our nearest and dearest?

Does Dr. Gervinus know anyone who will make such a reply to a posthumous charge against him of dulness and lack of humour ?

Elliot Stock, Paternoster Row, London.